Cathe

A Re

By

Jo Cooper

best wishes

With illustrations by Maria Ward

Jo Cooper

A Red Sky

A Red Sky by Jo Cooper
ISBN 9798798961887

First Published in 2022 by Jo Cooper

Copyright © 2022 Jo Cooper

Acknowledgements

I wish to record my thanks to my two
technical experts, **Damon Corr** who
advised me on matters concerning
working procedures for the Fire Service
during the war, and **Tony Gale**, who was
aged nine when the war began on the
island. His input of his memories as a child
during the war years has been invaluable.
I also wish to thank my niece **Clare Louise
Bennison** whose idea it was that I wrote
fiction, my daughter, **Mandy Meadows,** a
well-known isle of Wight photographer
who advised me on matters concerning
publishing, and finally my husband **Robert**
who has encouraged me throughout.

DEDICATION

This book is dedicated to my father Charles Brian Drawbridge and all the men of the Fire Service, who stood bravely fighting fires as bombs fell around them during the Second World War.

A RED SKY

CONTENTS

1.
Being Alright

'How do you feel?' people all around her were constantly asking. Lindy stood quietly in the graveyard. Her mother used to tell her how to behave at important events like this one. What was she supposed to say? What was she supposed to do? Her mother would have told her but she was no longer there. There was no one to tell her. Lindy turned around.

'So young to lose her mother,' someone said. 'Kitty was a wonderful woman,' came from another woman. 'Such a nice person, so nice,' a lady said to a group who had gathered around Lindy.

Lindy shrugged her shoulders and gave them a short false smile. Her mouth turned up at the corners, independent of the rest of her face. She really did not know how she felt. She did not know herself. How was she supposed to feel? She wasn't ill. That is what people say when you are ill, 'How do you feel?' She didn't hurt anywhere but there was this feeling of utter and complete sadness.

A gap appeared in the crowd and she caught sight of her father. She ran to him and grabbed his hand. 'Alright my darling?' he said. Lindy nodded her head; she was fine now as she was holding her father's hand.

I am alright, she mused to herself, *I will be alright. Mummy has gone but she said that I would be alright. So, I will be alright.*

As they walked along, Lindy became aware of the bright blue sky. 'Look up, Lindy!' she heard her mother say, 'I shall be in the blue sky, in the trees, the birds and all the beauty around. I will not be on the ground. When you see a robin, take a long look, that might be me.' The 10-year-old did as she was told, and looked up.

The party slowly walked back to their house where there was a high tea laid out. It was late in January 1940 and food rationing had just been brought in earlier that month. Friends of the family had clubbed together and brought plates of nice things to eat.

'What a lovely spread!' said her father, William, as he turned around and looked at their friends. 'Thank you so much. It all looks delicious. Don't you think so, Lindy?'

Lindy held tightly to her father's hand. She didn't want any food. She didn't want anything, just her daddy. She wanted to be alone with him.

'Alright, my darling?' he said again. Lindy nodded her head again. 'We will be alright, won't we?' she whispered.

William bent his knees and crouched down so he was eye to eye in line with Lindy. 'Of course, sweetheart,' he reassured her. 'We will be fine; you are your mother's daughter. She was strong and we will be strong just like her.' He turned and stood up to make some remark or other in reply to the endless rubbishy talk, the usual platitudes that everyone was making.

Strong, thought Lindy, *Mummy wasn't strong enough to get better. It wasn't fair. What is this cancer?*

2

Why did she have to get it? Why did she have to leave us? How did she know that she was not going to get better and that she was going to …? She shuddered at the word; she didn't even want to think it. *I must be strong. I will be strong.*

Her life had been good. To make the most of their time together during the summer school holidays, Lindy and her mother often went down to Southsea Common, met her father after work, sat and watched the sunset. As it went down the sky often turned red. 'Red sky at night, shepherds' delight,' said William. 'That's what they say don't they?'

'But where are the shepherds? There are no sheep in Portsmouth,' said Lindy and Kitty together.

'You always say that!' Kitty chastised her husband.

'That red sky is our delight,' William suggested, 'and we'll all be safe under the red sky.'

The family sat together, cuddled up close, as the sun went down. 'Time for bed,' said Kitty. The three walked home hand in hand.

'I've so much enjoyed your summer holiday this year, Lindy,' said Kitty. 'Have you, darling?'

Lindy returned to her boarding school, Oakleigh School for Girls after the summer holidays full of excitement and enthusiasm. She loved her school. She was doing well and found the work challenging but fun, especially when she got good marks for her essays. She loved to write. Kitty had loved reading her long letters, and returned an equal number of pages each time she wrote. They weren't full of boring stuff like who she had visited, or the committees she worked with, but full of happy news about her and her father. She always added some made-up story or other. They were often about the animals that lived nearby. Once, she made the rather large cat next door into a high court judge. In the dock that day was the yappy terrier that lived over the road. Lindy loved those stories.

Then in November her letters became shorter and less frequent. However much she tried to write jolly letters to her beloved daughter, it was impossible. Pain was beginning to take over her body and mind.

Lindy came home for Christmas, and afterwards it was decided that she should stay at home. She hadn't wanted to go back to school. All that was pointless now. What was important was her mother. Once Lindy had got over the news that her mother was so ill, she lifted herself up and went to sit with her. Kitty, despite looking tired and thin, managed to smile for her lovely daughter. Lindy hated it when she spoke about dying.

Every day Lindy said to herself *I must be strong*, which she was. She ran errands and helped her father nurse her mother. The nurse who came every day commented on how strong Lindy was, and how brave.

She helped wash her mother's face and hands, making sure that the soap she used was her favourite, and that the towel was the pretty one that she liked. She

4

brushed her long blonde hair that lay on the pillow. Nothing was too much for her. She even learnt how to cook some basic meals. Once, when she was not sure if the onions were done, she took the pan upstairs to her mother's bedroom to ask her opinion.

'What have we here?' asked her mother.

'Onions – I've fried them gently. Do you think they're done enough?'

Kitty laughed, and Lindy frowned. 'I want to make sure that I get it right.' Lindy said slightly indignantly.

Her mother stopped laughing and put on a serious face. 'Now let me look,' she said. She peered into the frying pan. 'Yes! I think they're just right. You have the makings of being a good cook. Well done!'

The last week was the worst. The pain was so intense, the district nurse gave Kitty more and more injections. They made her sleep. There were no long chats with Lindy anymore. The last words she said to her daughter were 'Be strong. You will be alright.'

Eventually she was asleep all the time. William was at her bedside constantly. He slept on the floor by her, and woke immediately Kitty made any noise. He talked to her a lot. He told her that he loved her and would always. 'My sweet, you have a wonderful daughter. You are so clever to have produced such a wonderful child.'

Lindy was a little embarrassed overhearing that. Then one day she heard him say 'I know you're in so much pain, Kitty. Go to sleep. You can leave us now. We will

5

be alright.'

Alright! That beastly word! Lindy thought. *It keeps turning up all the time.*

After Kitty died, the nurse tidied her golden hair and laid her back on the pillow. William found some pretty lace in the sewing box to put around her head. He had wanted some wild flowers, but there were none to pick in late January. She looked beautiful. All the anxiety had gone from her face.

'All the pain has gone now,' said the nurse.

The funeral tea dragged on for ages. Eventually the last guest left and Lindy was glad she had her father all to herself. They cleared away and washed up the last remaining cups and plates. They didn't speak at all. Neither knew what to say. They listened to the radio. Just before the nine o'clock news, he said, 'Time to go to bed, my precious. The blackouts are already up.' Lindy left the room quietly and went upstairs.

Later that night, she awoke and heard her father crying.

2.

Cludgy

Lindy did not go back to Oakleigh School for Girls. It was decided that it was best that she stay with her father. William's sister, Lindy's Aunt Joan, came to stay to help out for a while. Aunt Joan had never married. There was a rumour that she had had a fiancé who died in the Great War, but it was never spoken about. Her father, Lindy's grandfather, had made provision for her in his will, as it was felt that she would never marry and would need money to live as she aged. She was frugal, and consequently this made her wealthy enough not to have to earn a living, and she threw herself into her good and charitable works. She was very efficient and organised everything. She never ceased telling Lindy and her father so. 'There is a place for everything, and everything should be in that place,' was one of her favourite sayings. Lindy hated it when Aunt Joan went through Kitty's lovely clothes. They were of the finest quality. William worked for a large department store in Southsea as a floorwalker. He was able to choose the best items and get a discount on anything he bought.

'I've made three piles,' announced Aunt Joan, 'Those that might be useful for other members of the family; those that could be altered for Lindy; and those that were in such a poor condition that they needed to be thrown out and given to charity. Nothing should be wasted.

7

There **is** a war on you know! Not that you would notice it. People are calling it the Phoney War.'

'Yes, I know,' replied William not wanting to get into any discussion at all.

Getting no further response from William, Joan turned to her niece. 'Lindy! What do you think? Does it feel like we are at war?'

Lindy shrugged her shoulders and gave Aunt Joan a short false smile. She had used those a lot lately. She had no opinion on the 'Phoney War'. She didn't care about anything. Her life was a total contrast from what it had been before. Even when her mother was so ill, the house was filled with noise of one sort or another.

'I like to hear you romping around the house,' her mother had said. All of that was gone; her father was quiet, lost in his own thoughts. He was at a loss to know what to do or how to do it.

Arrangements were made for Lindy to attend the local day school. Finding a school uniform to match her new school was thought to be unnecessary. Aunt Joan decreed that she had a perfectly serviceable set of school clothes from her old school. 'Waste not, want not, that's what I say.' Her uniform was of the highest quality, purchased, with a discount, from the department store where her father worked. It comprised a fawn-coloured skirt, a cream-coloured shirt (referred to as gold), a brown tie with a gold streak running through it and a fawn-coloured jumper which had been knitted by Aunt Joan.

This new school was very different. Lindy, who had worked so hard at her boarding school, now changed completely. The work was not challenging, and she got bored very easily. She would drift off into her thoughts about her beloved mother and her darling father. She would often be told off for staring out of the window.

She was more advanced in her learning. She did as she was asked: she produced work which she did not think was very good, but which received very high marks and was top of the class. This did not go down well with the other children. To make matters worse her school clothes were different from the others. On the whole they took a dislike to this 'toffee nosed, clever dick girl in posh clothes.' There were over 30 children in her class. In September 1939 the classrooms had emptied as the children were evacuated. However, they had refilled when the pupils returned after nothing had happened and the 'Phoney War' dragged on.

The classroom full of 30 children was often very noisy until the teacher, Mr Hacker, came in holding his cane under his arm, as if he were a sergeant major in the army. The noise subsided. He stood erect and completely still. Then without warning he whacked his cane on the nearest desk and there was dead silence. He didn't have to say anything, he just stood there glaring. Needless to say, the children called him Mr 'Whacker'. No area was hidden from him as he marched about the classroom. His eyes were never still. No-one knew who he was looking at, or who he was going to pounce on next. He was in his early 50s, an experienced teacher and, apart from a spell in the army, he had taught junior schoolchildren for many years.

The desk he hit with his cane most was at the front. Seated there was Lucy Jones, a shy and timid little girl. She was very thin; and her clothes had been washed and worn many times. She wore a faded navy-blue tunic, the pleats of which had long disappeared at the back where she sat. For warmth she wore a thin cardigan, which had darns in the elbows, and was done up with a selection of buttons. Her wispy hair was pulled back into two plaits, which throughout the day became loose and wisps of hair fell over her face.

The class was arranged in order of standards: Lindy was at the back on the far right; and Lucy was at the front on the left. She was as quiet as a mouse. She said nothing. She didn't answer questions, as she was too terrified to give the wrong answer, and get laughed at by the teacher and the other children. It was her desk that Mr Hacker stood near, and it was her desk that got the whack from his cane. No-one knew when he was going to strike the desk, and it often caught Lucy by surprise. If she was leaning forward, she got the tip of the cane on her arm. She said nothing and never complained.

Lindy noticed this and thought it unfair. So, during lunch break, she went and sat with Lucy, and they became friends.

This arrangement was brought to the attention of the

10

teachers; Lindy asked if she could help Lucy during lessons and she was moved to a desk next to her. This suited both Mr Hacker and Lindy well. Lindy had a purpose in helping her new friend, whilst Mr Hacker didn't have to find work of the higher standard for this clever pupil. Knowing of her bereavement circumstances Mr Hacker moved his position and avoided hitting either girl's desk, and went to the desk at the opposite end of the line.

The two girls benefited from this. Lindy was happy when she was helping someone else, and Lucy was happy as she now had more confidence to answer questions in class, as she had asked Lindy if it was correct first. Academically Lindy didn't learn much during this time. Lucy, however, improved immensely.

At home, the most important time of day was when the BBC News was broadcast. This was transmitted throughout the day: at eight o'clock in the morning; one and six o'clock in the afternoon and finally nine o'clock in the evening. Aunt Joan always announced this and insisted that Lindy was quiet. She obviously hadn't noticed that Lindy was saying very little nor making any sound anyway.

The Phoney War continued until, in April 1940, Adolf Hitler invaded Denmark and Norway. He blitzed Belgium and Holland: their Queen Wilhelmina managed to escape to England to live in exile. In May the Germans occupied The Hague and were also just 60 miles from Paris. At the beginning of April, William resigned from the department store knowing that he would be conscripted. He decided that he wanted to stay in Portsmouth, so he chose to join the fire service. Aunt Joan finally left.

Winston Churchill became Prime Minister on the 10th of May. 'We'll be fine now that Winnie is in charge,' William reassured his daughter. His assurance was misplaced, and the situation worsened on the other side of the channel.

The decision was made to evacuate Lindy to safety when the British Army were cut off and stranded at Dunkirk in Northern France towards the end of May.

'Lindy,' her father said quite seriously, 'I must get you away from Portsmouth. The Germans will want to bomb us before they try to invade. You must go away to safety, but I must stay here and help.'

Lindy was speechless and tears rushed into her eyes.

'I won't be far away; just a ferry ride,' he said. 'I've found a place for you on the Isle of Wight. If needs be, I'll be on the first ferry to come over and find you. Through contacts at the store, I found a very nice lady and gentleman who live in a small village. They used to be in service. She was a cook, a very good one, so I'm told, and maid of all works. He was the gardener.'

William put his strong arms around his daughter and cuddled her close to him. 'It shouldn't be for a long time. Just until the immediate danger is over. I'll try to come over to see you when I get leave. And we can write to each other. My letters won't be quite as good as

Mummy's were, but I will try very hard.'

He paused and moved her, so he was looking at her full face. 'We must be strong, my darling.'

She packed her suitcase as she had done when she travelled to her boarding school. She attended her Portsmouth school for just one more day, wanting to say goodbye to Lucy. She took Lucy's address and promised to write and send her details of where she was living.

'We must keep in touch,' Lindy said.

'Yes of course,' Lucy replied through her tears. 'You're my best friend!'

On Monday 27th of May 1940 Lindy slung her gas mask box over her head and shoulder so it lay neatly across her body. With her suitcase in her hand, she boldly marched out of her house behind her father to take the bus to Portsmouth Harbour. She had travelled alone to Oakleigh school in Brighton on many occasions, but on the train, she met up with school friends, and there would be a bus waiting for them when they arrived at the station. She wondered who would meet her when she got to Ryde. She did not cry. *I must be strong*, she told herself. Her tummy felt twisted and she felt slightly sick.

She was dressed in her school uniform and had a label tied to her top buttonhole. 'Surely Daddy I don't need this. I didn't have one when I travelled to Brighton on my own.'

'You are going to be met by a lady from the Red Cross at the Pier Head, and I was told to put the label on so you'll

13

be easily recognised,' said her father. 'I want to be sure you are safe; you are so precious to me.'

'I love you Daddy,' Lindy said. She sniffed back the tears that were about to fall.

'Be strong for me,' was all that William could manage to utter.

'You must look after yourself Daddy, and don't get hurt.'

'Not if I can help it,' he laughed.

Why are you laughing? Lindy thought to herself. *If he came with me, we could be both safe together.*

'I must do my bit,' William continued. 'I'm a fireman now. I must help people when they're in trouble.'

A strange hand took her suitcase as Lindy walked up the narrow green gangplank onto the Isle of Wight Ferry.

'Where shall I put your case, Miss?' asked the seaman who had carried it.

Lindy was staring at her father. 'I beg your pardon. What did you say?'

'Your case, Miss, where shall I put it?'

'Oh! I'll have it with me please.' William was still there watching and waiting for the paddle steamer to leave. In silence they watched the men take down the gangplanks and untie the ropes, then the ferry moved away from the pier. Lindy watched and watched her father until she couldn't see him anymore. He continued to wave until the boat and Lindy were completely out of sight.

14

She found a seat behind her, picked up her suitcase and sat down. It was cold on deck. She remembered how she used to love the trips to the Isle of Wight with her mum and dad. The ferry ride was part of the excitement. Then there was the beach, the sandcastles, the cool seawater and the ice creams.

In no time it seemed that the boat arrived at the end of the pier. Men threw the ropes that tied the ferry to the stout bollards, then green gangplanks were lifted into place. Lindy was at the front of the queue to disembark. One of the seamen took her case again, as she climbed onto the gangplank. She took the case back and then looked up, and there in front of her was a lady dressed in Red Cross uniform.

'Hello Lindy. I'm Miss Vaughan, Peggy Vaughan. I am so pleased to meet you.'

Lindy was struck by her clear voice and formal approach. Lindy presented her hand. 'How do you do?' she said, just as her mother had taught her.

'I'm here to take you to your billet. It's in a little village not far, but we have to catch a bus and of course a tram to get us to the end of the pier. Give me your case, I'll carry that.'

They rushed across the wide concourse of the Pier Head to where the tram was. They climbed in and sat down on the wooden slatted seats. 'Not very comfortable,' said Peggy, 'but it's only a short journey. We'll be there in no time. Tell me about yourself.'

15

'There's not a lot to tell really.' The tram lurched to a start and then jogged its way down the length of the pier.

'The pier is half a mile long!' said Peggy trying to make some sort of conversation with her new charge.

Lindy was at a loss as to what she should say. Should she comment on the length of the pier or tell her all about herself. Where should she begin, there was so much to tell. She was just about to open her mouth to speak when Peggy said 'Oh! Here we are, I told you it was short!'

From the tram they walked to the bus stop. There were lots of green buses lined up along the Esplanade. At the far end Lindy could just see a train was emerging from the tunnel, billowing its smoke and tooting its whistle.

'It's a train, I'd forgotten about that. Are there any trolley buses here?' asked Lindy.

'No, there's too much country. They would get in the way of the trees!' said Peggy

They got on a Number 1a bus and Peggy put Lindy's case in the luggage rack. She looked reassuringly at Lindy. 'We won't forget it. I promise.'

'So Lindy, what do you like to do? Did you have a favourite subject at school?'

'When I was at Oakleigh, my boarding school in Brighton, I loved English. I used to write long letters to my mother. But she died.' Lindy stopped. She didn't want to say anymore.

'I know, I was told about your mother.' The

16

conductor stood beside them. 'One and a half to the bottom of Little Bridge Hill please.'

As they approached their stop the conductor kindly got Lindy's case out of the luggage rack. Peggy took it and they both got off the bus.

'Thank you.' Peggy called out.

'Yes, thank you very much,' Lindy politely added.

'That's alright me dears!' the conductor shouted out as he pressed the bell for the driver to hear, and the bus moved off.

Together they walked along a lane that twisted and turned. There were trees on both sides. 'Are we going through some woods?' Lindy asked.

'Well, I suppose it looks like that, there are lots of woods around here. I am sure you'll be allowed to play in some. If you look over there on your right, you'll see there are deep quarries. That is where they took out stone for building houses and the old abbey. It was also used in a cathedral on the mainland, so I'm told.'

There was a narrowing of the road and then they turned right. 'This is my church,' Peggy said. 'The cottage where you will be staying is just next door. Literally next door.'

In front of them in the narrow lane was a row of pretty cottages. There were plants in the small garden in front of the buildings.

Coming out of a gate opposite the cottage was a plump lady. A happy smiling face was framed by a mass of curly hair. She wore a bright blue flowery dress with an apron over the top. Her hands were grubby with soil. She spotted Lindy.

'Here she is!' she called out.

Peggy waved. 'Good afternoon, Mrs Sparrow.'

'And you must be Lindy,' said Mrs Sparrow. 'I'm so glad to meet you.'

'Hello Mrs Sparrow,' Lindy said quietly. She was a little overwhelmed by this large lady with a loud voice.

'Come on in, I've got your room all ready for you. Peggy, do you want to come in for a cup of tea?'

'No thanks, I must get home to my father, he's unwell again. I'll leave you here, Lindy, with Mrs Sparrow. Is that alright?'

Despite being a little unsure, Lindy boldly replied, 'Yes, of course.'

'Yes of course we'll be alright. Won't we dear?' Mrs Sparrow added.

There was that word again, Lindy thought. *Alright!*

During the next hour, Lindy unpacked her suitcase. 'Here is my ration book and some cheese, Daddy said that I was to give it to you.'

'Do you like cheese?' Mrs Sparrow asked.

'Oh yes, very much.'

'Perhaps I can teach you how to make it, one day. I often make butter, but not a lot.'

Mrs Sparrow showed Lindy around the house and introduced her to the new inside bathroom, which had a lavatory in it. This was a luxury and none of the other cottages in the block had one. Mrs Sparrow was very proud of it. 'So nice on a cold night, not having to go out and over the drive to the lavatory in the walled garden.'

There were three rooms downstairs, all with windows at the front and back. There was a kitchen with a table to eat at. Next to that was a more formal dining room. The last room was the sitting room. Although not lit, there was a large fireplace with logs laid ready in case the weather turned cold. 'I've known many a cold night in May and June. I must be prepared,' Mrs Sparrow explained.

That evening they had a light supper of homemade vegetable soup, crunchy bread, also made by Mrs Sparrow, followed by bread-and-butter pudding.

'Thank you, Mrs Sparrow,' Lindy said politely but honestly. 'That was delicious!'

'Now, Lindy, I'm not used to all this Mrs Sparrow, what do you want to call me? Some of the evacuees call their hosts Aunt or Auntie.'

Remembering her stiff and starchy Aunt Joan, Lindy didn't like that. She pulled a face.

'Right' she said. 'My full name before I was married was Clara Rudge, and at school I was nicknamed Cludgy. Would you like to call me Cludgy? All my friends do, I mean those that know me well.'

'Oh yes please, I like that. Cludgy! Thank you.'

19

3
Arthur and the Allotments

Cludgy's husband was not blessed with an unusual or sweet nickname. He was simply Arthur Sparrow. He had been the head gardener at the big house behind the church and Cludgy had been cook and maid of all work in the same house. In 1938 he turned 65 and retired at the end of that year. However, in September of the following year when war was declared, there was a need for experienced gardeners. Arthur was just that. He had grown flowers and vegetables for over fifty years starting when he was just 14 years old.

Many areas of land were dug up for growing vegetables. Arthur was in his element; he was an expert and very sought after. Rose-beds went out with the spade, to be replaced by potatoes. Pristine lawns that once were used for garden parties were now planted up with all sorts of vegetables. Arthur knew how to grow these and to use the land to the best advantage. At the big house they even dug up the croquet lawn to house a goat for fresh milk and cheese.

Arthur was a warden of the Air Raid Precaution or ARP, and he did his fair share of duties in Little Bridge and the surrounding areas. He was not at home when Lindy arrived. He had been giving advice to a group of potential gardeners on the other side of the village, and from there he had gone straight on to do his shift with the ARP.

With him was his trusty dog Texi. They returned home at 11 o'clock.

'All quiet?' asked his wife.

'Yep! Not a sound, no lights showing,' he said as he sat down and took his boots off. 'Here Cludgy listen,' Arthur said, 'I was walking Texi down Ladies Lane when at the bottom of the hill he turned off to the right and bounded down to the beach as he usually does. I followed him and when I reached the shore, I spotted some boats all heading along the Solent towards Portsmouth. I couldn't see where they were going, but it was strange. They were all motorised boats. You know, ones used for fishing or for boat trips in the summer. What I want to know is, where did they get their petrol from and why? I reckon there's something going on. Charlie Robins at the ARP post said his neighbour has been asked to go and take his boat, the Sallyann, to help transport something or someone to somewhere. It's all very hush hush.'

'Careless talk cost lives,' Cludgy snapped. 'It is not for us to know. When we need to be told, we will be. Now - no more!' She finished heating up his soup and poured it into a bowl. Arthur sat down and ate his meal with some crusty bread and followed it with his portion of bread-and-butter pudding, which was now cold.

'Yep! I suppose you're right. But there's no one here who is a spy, is there?' said Arthur defending himself.

'That's not the point!'

'Did our evacuee arrive alright?'

21

'Yes,' said Cludgy in a whisper. 'She's probably asleep now. Don't wake her, whatever you do.'

Lindy had gone to bed at eight. She had sat with Cludgy and told her all about herself, her school and what subjects she liked the most. 'I like writing and English Language lessons the best! Maths I find a bit hard, but I manage, and as for drawing, I'm no good at that at all.'

Cludgy sat quietly, her knitting needles clicking away. She paused, put her work on her lap and mused, 'I used to like drawing but found English a little difficult. Each of us have our talents. I can draw what I see, and you can describe what you see in words and phrases. We all have our gifts.'

'I used to write to Mummy a lot, and she used to write back.' Lindy stopped and became silent. She felt tears come to her eyes, so she took a deep breath and sat up straight. *I must be strong,* Lindy thought.

Cludgy waited until she felt the moment was right. 'I know, your father told me all about your letters. She was a lovely mum, wasn't she?'

'I think I'd like to go to bed now, please. How do I put the blackouts up?' Lindy spoke briefly and to the point.

'That's already done my love. Now you know where everything is.' Cludgy got up. 'Did you find the towel I left for you? There's a bowl and jug of water for you in your room where you can give yourself a quick wash. Now anything else you want you just tell Cludgy, and I'll get it for you. Night night then.' Cludgy wanted to give her a

22

cuddle and a kiss good night, but she could see Lindy was not ready for that.

Lindy turned around. 'Good night Cludgy. Thank you for having me to stay in your lovely house.'

Cludgy gulped. It was a good thing that the lights were low as she was near to tears herself.

Every effort had been made to ensure Lindy's room was pretty. As well as a comfortable bed with a pretty bedspread, there was a four-drawer chest of drawers on which there was the enamel bowl and jug. There was a chair on which Lindy laid her clothes near to the chest of drawers. Across the corner of the room Arthur had rigged a wardrobe. He had fixed a pole across the corner on the picture rails, on which was a curtain made by Cludgy. Behind this was another rail for hanging clothes. There were two coat hangers.

'If you need any more coat hangers, I'll get them for you,' Cludgy had said earlier that day.

Lindy only had her school uniform and gabardine mac. 'No thank you,' she replied, 'I have enough.'

She slept well. There was no noise at night except the odd screech of an owl. She was warm and comfortable in her bed.

Next morning Lindy met Arthur. As soon as Lindy walked into the kitchen she was greeted with Arthur's lovely smile. First of all, Lindy noticed his two piercing blue eyes, then his mass of bushy untidy hair that outlined his handsome, wrinkled and weather-beaten face. He wore a navy-blue jumper, which was tucked into a pair of baggy trousers held up by a big leather belt. Despite his age, he was upright, fit and strong.

Sitting at the side of Arthur was a dog. 'His name is Texi,' he said. Texi rose up, looked at Lindy and growled. 'That's enough, Texi!' snapped Arthur as he stroked his head. The dog settled. Arthur looked at his dog and said 'This is Lindy, you are to be nice to her. She is our guest.' Lindy stood still almost waiting for instructions as to what to do next.

'What sort of dog is he?' she asked.

'A very nice one,' joked Arthur.

'No, I'm sorry, I mean what sort of breed of dog?' Lindy replied.

'Oh!' he said teasingly, 'I don't know. I think he's a bitza.'

Cludgy butted in. 'Arthur, stop teasing her!'

'Sorry for teasing you Lindy! He's a mongrel, bits of this breed and bits of that breed! A bitza! It's a joke. Do you get it?'

Arthur gave Lindy a piece of crust from his toast. 'Lay it on your flattened hand and give it to Texi.' Lindy crouched down and as instructed put out her hand flat and Texi took the crust. She stroked him, and he turned his head around and looked at her. Lindy loved him.

'I can see you are going to be great friends,' said Cludgy.

Arthur looked at Lindy and half closed his eyes. 'Oh!

24

I see you want to take my faithful friend away from me,' he said.

'No, I'm sorry, I … I … didn't mean to take him from you.' Lindy was slightly embarrassed.

'It's alright, we will share him. He can take no end of stroking and cuddling,' Arthur said.

'And long walks!' Cludgy added.

Texi was a scruffy mongrel dog. The hair on his back was a light tan colour, also coarse and rough. His head was smooth. He had a happy face and, as he looked up at Lindy, she sensed that he was pleased to see her.

'Now my dear' said Cludgy, 'would you like to come with me to feed the chickens and see if any hens have laid, so we can have eggs for breakfast?'

This was a new experience for Lindy. She understood that eggs came from chickens, but had never met one.

'Texi has to stay in-doors,' Cludgy said. 'He has a tendency to bounce about and upset the hens.' They went out of the kitchen door together. Lindy was carrying a basket lined with straw. They walked around the side of the house and across the lane. Cludgy opened the gate, and instructed Lindy to shut it.

'All country gates must be shut,' she said. 'It's to keep any animals in and dogs out.'

'Won't the chickens just go under the gate?' Lindy asked.

'Of course, they would, but they have their own enclosure and the wire-netting for that has been sunken

25

into the earth. That's to stop the foxes and badgers digging as they try to get in.'

They walked across the field, through the rows of vegetables and into the wired off hen enclosure, where they saw the solidly built hen house. 'My Arthur made that,' she announced proudly. 'Clever, don't you think?'

Lindy was surprised how long it took for Cludgy to gain entry into the hen house. Firstly, she removed a large and very heavy plank of wood that was slotted into two robust hooks. Once detached a low but stout door was revealed. This was fitted with a strong bolt. Cludgy slid the bolt, opened the door and out poured six white chickens.

'Would you like to scatter their breakfast on the ground?' said Cludgy. 'They'll leave me alone as I go and check for eggs.'

Attached to the main construction was a big box at the side on top of which lay a large piece of wood. This was fixed by sliding the plank through two large oblong metal hoops secured to the shed.

'There are a lot of locks, bolts and planks of wood to keep the chickens from escaping,' remarked Lindy.

'Oh no, the locks are not there to prevent the chickens from leaving, they are there to keep the foxes and badgers out. That's if they've been able to get through the sunken wire-netting fence. Foxes will kill and eat the chickens. Badgers will also kill them, but they're after the eggs.'

26

Lindy had finished scattering the hens' food on the ground. She turned to Cludgy.

'Open the lid Lindy and see if they've given you some breakfast.'

Lindy lifted up the lid and squealed with delight. Lying in the straw in individual sections were six white eggs.

'Light Sussex Hens always lay white eggs,' Cludgy informed her.

With the eggs placed carefully in the basket, they walked back to the cottage.

'How would you like me to cook your eggs?'

Lindy eyes lit up. She loved eggs.

'You may have two today because it's a special day!' continued Cludgy.

'Oh, thank you,' said Lindy. 'A special day? Is it someone's birthday?'

'No, it's because today is Lindy's first breakfast with Cludgy. And I think that is worth celebrating!'

A big beam came over Lindy's face. She was flattered. She felt safe here. She felt loved too.

'Please could you boil them for me? And can I have them with toasted soldiers?'

4

Reggie

Lindy enjoyed her breakfast immensely. It was obvious to Cludgy that she had. 'Can we go hunting for eggs tomorrow Cludgy, please?' Lindy asked.

'They may not lay so well tomorrow, but of course you can help me with the hens. We must remember that we barter with some of the eggs. Betsy Brown next door had a lot of flour left but needed eggs, so we did a swap.' Betsy was Cludgy's nearest neighbour and a close friend.

'Have you had enough to eat my dear?' Cludgy asked.

'Yes, thank you,' Lindy politely replied.

'I've arranged for you to start at the village school this afternoon. We will walk around together but then I expect you to walk back by yourself.'

Lindy was not looking forward to another Mr Hacker and a large noisy classroom. Cludgy recognised her trepidation.

'It's a lovely school. I know one of the teachers. He plays the organ at church. What worries you about the school? I'm sure you will get on fine a clever girl like yourself.'

'Oh, it's not the work,' replied Lindy. 'I can more than cope with that!'

'Well! What is it then?'

'I don't know really,' she replied, not wanting to be a nuisance. 'I'll manage.'

28

'The evacuee who lives next door to us goes to the same school, you can walk home with him. His name is Reggie. He comes from Portsmouth too. He came over in September but, unlike a lot of the children, he has stayed. He is 10 years old like you,' Cludgy went on.

The rest of the morning was spent helping in the garden, weeding between the rows of carrots and onions. There was a wall opposite the kitchen window. There had been gates, but they had been taken for salvage. The stone wall surrounded another garden.

Arthur went fishing from the beach. Just before lunch Lindy started writing a letter to her father. She told him all about the journey and people she had met.

At lunch time all three of them and Texi sat down together. Cludgy had made baked potatoes and had added some butter. She had grated the cheese which Lindy had brought from home and put that on top.

'That'll keep you going until you come home from school,' she said.

'Did you see any more boats Arthur whilst you were fishing?' Cludgy asked her husband, knowing full well that he went fishing in the hope of seeing just that.

'No nothing at all,' he sighed. 'I could see very little of the area around Portsmouth either.'

'I bet you took your binoculars. You will get yourself into trouble - people will say that you're a spy!' teased Cludgy.

'I use them when I'm with the ARP.'

29

'That's different and you know it!' she warned.

Lindy dressed in her fawn school uniform, picked up her gas-mask-box and placed it over her head and shoulder. She stepped boldly out of the kitchen door and started the long walk to school.

'Ah good!' said Cludgy. 'You've remembered your gas mask.'

Together they walked around the lane to where Lindy got off the bus the day before. They crossed the main road and walked up the lane, which had a cemetery on the left-hand side. Lindy looked and saw the cold grey gravestones and she shuddered! She looked up, straight ahead, and strode firmly to the top of the road where the school stood on the right. The playground was full of noisy children. A football was being kicked around. There were children throwing small balls against a wall.

Lindy followed Cludgy up the steps and through a large door which was covered with flaking green paint. She turned to her right and climbed up again into a large classroom. Seated behind a desk was a grey-haired lady reading a document.

'Hello, Mrs Sparrow, I see you've brought Lindy with you,' she said. They shook hands. 'Tell me Lindy, how have you settled in with Mr and Mrs Sparrow?'

'Very nicely, thank you,' Lindy replied.

'I'm so glad. Now you are going to join us for a while. My name is Simons, Miss Simons. I have a report from your last school and also one from your boarding school,

Oakleigh in Brighton. Your father sent them. He wanted to make sure you are happy. I see from the headmistress at your Brighton school that you were doing very well. Good … good … that is good.'

The next few minutes were filled with writing Lindy's details on a form and entering her name into the register, together with her starting date at the school.

'Right,' said Miss Simons, 'that's all done. You can go and join the other children in the playground. There's only a short time left of the lunch break.'

Lindy returned to the playground and stood at the top looking around. Cludgy followed her. Lindy looked very smart in her Brighton boarding school uniform. Dressed in her brown-coloured skirt with three pleats, her cream blouse and a brown-coloured knitted jumper, she stood out. The colour she had been told in Brighton was fawn. She had stout shoes and fawn long socks. Looking at her charge, Cludgy realised just how out of place she looked. All the other children had clothes of navy blue.

Just then a small, skinny, scruffy boy came up to her.

'Hello!' he said. 'I'm Reggie. I live next door to Cludgy and Arthur. I live with Betsy and Robert Brown. I call her Auntie Bee. We could walk home together if you like. I come from Portsmouth too.'

Reggie reminded her of a lot of the boys in Portsmouth. Above his cheery smile and cheeky expression his hair seemed to have a mind of its own and stuck out in a random manner. He wore ill-fitting grey

31

shorts, which hung on a pair of old braces, so that they hung on his hips and came down to his knees. His grey socks were round his ankles, so several wounds and grazes on his legs were revealed.

'My goodness,' asked Lindy, 'where did you get all those injuries?'

'Well,' announced Reggie, as if he were going into an important speech. He pointed to them individually. 'I got this one last Wednesday, or was it Thursday, falling over playing football in the playground. But I got up straight away and scored a goal.'

'That was good!' Lindy said.

'This one I got falling down in the woods near the beach. Did you know that there are old quarries around here? I fell down in one of those too.'

'How do you get on with the other boys?' asked Lindy.

'They are alright. I think they like me, because I'm good at kicking a football really hard, and I make them laugh! I don't think Miss Simons likes me much. She says I am...,' he paused and took a long breath and announced, 'dis**T**ruptive.'

Just then the bell rang, and all the children ran to their lines. Reggie waited until the lines were nearly full and then showed Lindy where to go. At the command of the teacher, and after there was '**complete silence**', they filed into the building. Class 1 were first to walk in, followed by class 2 and so on, until the playground was empty.

Miss Simons showed Lindy where to sit and handed her an exercise book and a pencil. 'Do you have your own ink pen, Lindy?' Lindy nodded. 'Perhaps you could bring it in tomorrow to use. We're a little short of pens.'

As in Portsmouth, Lindy was seated at the back on the right, but there was no window to look out of. Reggie was in the front row.

They were handed a picture from a magazine and told to write a story about what they saw in the picture. Lindy's picture was an advertisement for Macleans toothpaste. A girl was photographed behind a closed window with her mouth shut. There was sticky tape across the window to prevent the glass from shattering. The next picture had her with both the window and her mouth open.

Lindy contemplated whether to write the actual story of the advertisement, or make something up about the girl. She chose the latter. She thought for a moment, and then with her mind whizzing around she wrote a story about a lady looking for a friend and seeing her through the window. She wrote fast and soon filled up two pages of her exercise book. She looked around at the others in the classroom. No-one had filled a page yet. Lindy slowed down. She remembered the children in the school in Portsmouth and being called 'a know-it-all in posh clothes.'

At the end of the day, the children filed out of the

classroom and down the steps into the playground. A boy pushed Lindy and she fell down the steps. Her heart sank as she overheard one girl say to another, 'Ooh look at her in her posh clothes. She wrote two pages this afternoon. I bet it was all rubbish!' Then, as she was picking herself up, she heard 'Don't you hurt my friend, or I'll punch you!' Reggie was standing up as tall as he could, looking up at a boy who was much taller and bigger than him.

The boy moved away just as Miss Simons came into the playground. Reggie remained looking stern and standing still.

'He's a bully,' said Reggie, 'and you need to stand up to him. He's been having a go at me for ages. It started with him patting me on the head when we stood in queues, then he put dirt in my hair. The last thing was he put a worm on my head!'

'Oh! How horrid!' gasped Lindy.

'Anyway, that's why now I get to the back of the row so he can't be behind me. I'm always the last one in the line to walk into class.'

'I'm not sure you would've come off best if he'd fought you,' said Lindy.

'Nah! My dad taught me how to box proper. I can look after me-self I can.'

'Don't you mean properly?' Lindy said, correcting him.

'Yeah!' he shouted as he made a grimace and posed as a fighter in a boxing ring. 'I know how to punch and

34

where to punch, and he doesn't! See, I can box proper! Me dad taught me.'

They started walking home more or less in silence. Lindy tried to break the silence. 'How did you get on with your story this afternoon?'

'I didn't write much, I never do. I don't like writing stories.'

'I wrote rather a lot,' Lindy said. But then she thought that sounded like boasting.

They turned the corner towards the church and Reggie suddenly ran on ahead. 'Did you know that there were smugglers in Little Bridge?'

'No, I didn't!' Lindy shouted back.

'Yeah, there's a gravestone of one of them in there. I'll show you tomorrow. Bye'

Reggie charged ahead and disappeared in the front door of the house where he was staying.

'Bye!' Reggie shouted again as he slammed the door. Lindy quietly walked into the kitchen where she found Cludgy sitting unpicking Arthur's navy jumper.

5
Fitting In

On the table were pieces of Arthur's navy-blue jumper.

'What are you doing?' asked Lindy, 'Didn't I see Arthur wearing that this morning?'

'Remember how I told you all about bartering?'

'Yes?' said Lindy, trying to work out how a navy-blue jumper in pieces could be used for swapping.

'I'm going to make you a navy-blue jumper for school.'

'But I have a school jumper. There's nothing wrong with it. Aunt Joan made it!'

'There is one thing wrong with it. Can you guess?'

Lindy couldn't think. There were no holes in it. It wasn't saggy or worn anywhere.

'No, I can't guess.'

'Your jumper is brown in colour, and all the children wear navy-blue. So, I am going to knit you a navy-blue jumper, and Arthur's jumper is just the right colour.'

'How can that be barter? He won't fit in mine!'

'No, of course not. But the brown one will also be unpicked and made into a jumper with some navy-blue features! You know, I'll do the cuffs and a stripe out of leftover navy-blue wool from his old one! As I made it in the first place I've also some navy-blue wool left over.' Cludgy looked up and smiled, obviously pleased with her ingenuity. 'Now I'm going to need your help.'

'Of course, what do you want me to do?'

'I've put a stew in the oven. Could you please peel the potatoes and carrots?'

'Of course!' Lindy replied.

'I'll show you how.'

'It's alright, Cludgy, my mum taught me lots about cooking. I can peel potatoes and carrots.'

Cludgy beamed, as she didn't want to leave her unpicking.

'And then you can help me with the jumper. Go and get changed out of your fawn jumper, I want to keep it as clean as possible. Bring it down with you and I'll show you how to unpick it. I'll want to wash the wool when it has been unpicked.'

'I've got a green cardigan that I use for play,' Lindy suggested, 'I can wear that one.'

After she had prepared the vegetables, Lindy picked up the brown school jumper ready to start work. She felt a little guilty, as Aunt Joan had made such a fuss when she was knitting it. She repeatedly proclaimed that as she was an expert knitter: it was to be the best knitted jumper she would ever own. Cludgy showed Lindy how to find the stitches that held the garment together and then how to find the end stitch in the knitting to start to unravel it. Sitting behind a high-backed chair, Lindy started to unravel Auntie Joan's knitting and wind the wool around the chair-back.

When Arthur came home the kitchen was a hive of

industry. He was wearing the same trousers, but had a dark brown jumper on. Lindy had peeled the vegetables, which were waiting to be cooked. Cludgy and Lindy were sitting with a chair back facing them. Pieces of Arthur's navy-blue and Lindy's brown jumper were on their laps as they pulled the stitches undone and then wound the wool around the backs of the chairs. A piece of Arthur's navy-blue jumper fell on the floor. Texi picked it up and shook it hard as he growled. 'Texi, drop it at once!' commanded Arthur. Texi had no intention of dropping it, neither at once nor at any other time. He continued to kill the navy-blue sleeve.

'Don't pull it out of his mouth, I want the wool in as good condition as possible. Give him a biscuit and he should drop the knitting.' Cludgy was right. As soon as Texi spotted the biscuit he dropped the sleeve, ready for Lindy to quickly snatch it up out of his way.'

'You didn't waste much time getting started on your plan. We only talked about it this morning and I've only been out since ten,' said Arthur.

'Oh Arthur, I never thought …' Lindy said. 'I hope you don't mind!'

'Not at all,' Arthur said. 'I'm looking forward to my new brown jumper with navy features!'

Lindy continued working, enjoying every minute as Cludgy finished cooking the dinner. It was difficult to stop Lindy from her task. Space was made on the table to lay it for dinner. Lindy gulped down her food as fast as she could.

'Slow down, you'll get indigestion!' Cludgy warned.

As his contribution towards the cottage industry, Arthur did the washing up and cleared away. It wasn't long before they finished unpicking the two jumpers. 'I'll need to wash this now,' said Cludgy 'so it's ready to be knitted.'

Cludgy put a strand of wool through the middle of each skein and tied it tight to stop them from unravelling. She took the skeins to the sink where she prepared a bowl of warm water with Lux flakes in it. She swished it around to make sure the flakes were dissolved. Gently she put in each skein, pressed it down, lifted it up and squeezed it. She repeated the process with all the wool.

'I can remember my mother doing this,' Cludgy said, gazing out of the window. 'I must get on! It'll be dark soon and I won't be able to see the washing line to hang them on.'

She rinsed the skeins in warm water and squeezed them out, firstly by hand, and then put them in a towel to get more moisture out. She disappeared out of the door into the failing light.

'I've hung them on hooks in the shed,' she said on her return. 'I didn't want all our hard work to be ruined if it had rained. Best to be safe rather than sorry.'

She sat down at the table and sighed. She was suddenly aware of her apprentice's eyes drooping.

'Gosh Lindy, look at the time! It's nearly time for the

nine o'clock news and your bedtime. Up you go. Well done we've worked well today.'

The news from France was not good. Lindy picked up words like 'Belgium, Holland and surrender'. She heard Arthur say something about 'extra ARP training owing to the threat ...' The effort of trying to hear the radio and their conversation, coupled with all the work she had done that day, led to Lindy falling asleep quickly.

The next day was Wednesday. The weather was fine, and Cludgy was able to move the wool to the washing line, which was bathed in sunshine.

Lindy dressed for school in her uniform and put on her old green cardigan. There were two darns on each elbow that her mother had done last summer. She rubbed them with her thumb and, shutting her eyes, she tried to picture her mother with her darning needle and wooden mushroom as she mended the sleeves. She held up the darn to her nose and tried to smell something that reminded her of her mother. There was nothing: Aunt Joan had washed it.

Wearing a cardigan with mended sleeves was more acceptable to the children in the class. There was no name calling. The children were given back their stories inspired by the magazine picture. Miss Simons had praised her work in front of the class. Remembering what the girl said yesterday, Lindy wished she hadn't made such a fuss. She was also embarrassed, as she didn't feel the work was that good at all. Miss Simons made no comment when she handed Reggie's three lines back to him.

At each break time, Reggie was at her side. At lunch time as the two children sat on the grass at the end of the playground. Lindy tentatively broached the subject of the English lesson. 'I'll give you a hand with your English if you like, I used to help a friend in Portsmouth and she ...'

'Can't be bothered,' Reggie butted in. 'Won't need it when I'm grown up, I'm going to work with my dad, and he can't read!'

Lindy thought of no end of things to say here that would enforce the need for reading and writing. She avoided them.

'Oh - what does he do?'

'This and that,' said Reggie. 'That's what my dad says he does - this and that.'

'Where is he now?'

'He's a prisoner.'

'A prisoner!' Lindy was astounded that he was taken as a prisoner of war so soon after war began.

The afternoon's lesson was geography. This usually meant learning about places in the world and in England, and what their main industry was. This was a little difficult as with Germany's various invasions the situation in each place was different. Miss Simons stuck to towns and places in England. At the end of the day, when the class were getting ready to go home, Lindy approached Miss Simons and asked, 'Where are Belgium and Holland? I heard the names on the news last night.'

41

Miss Simons took a map of Northern Europe and pointed to the countries. Lindy stared at the map. She then found the Isle of Wight. 'They're quite far apart, aren't they Miss Simons?'

'Yes,' reassured Miss Simons. 'They are quite a distance away. Now run along home Lindy, I've work to do.'

The walk home was interspersed with sudden bursts of Reggie's energy. He would run and then stop, turning to wait for Lindy to catch up.

'Come on slow coach!' he shouted.

When she got close to him, he delivered another piece of information about the lane. Lindy discovered that the large dips at the side of the road were in fact the quarries where stone had been taken to build the church, Quarr Abbey and a cathedral on the mainland.

'Peggy told me that yesterday,' she said.

'So, you know it's true then! Come on slow coach!'

She discovered where the rectory was, and that a large manorial house towards the end of the lane had been a former rectory.

As they turned the corner of the road just before the cottages, Lindy learnt that Reggie was starving and if he didn't get anything to eat, he would surely die!

'I'm sure you won't!' Lindy assured him.

Through the gate, Reggie ran to his door.

'Bye!' he shouted to Lindy.

Then 'Hello Auntie Bee!' as he disappeared into the

house, 'Got anything to eat? I'm starving!' He slammed the door.

Lindy walked into the kitchen to find Cludgy winding a skein into a ball of wool. She had made a start but balancing the skein on one of the knobs on the back of the chair was difficult.

'Would you like to help me, Lindy?' she asked.

'Shall I peel some vegetables?' Lindy offered.

'No, this is much more of an important job! Could you hold the skeins of wool in both hands apart so I can unwind the wool and make it into a ball.'

They got on like a house on fire. Cludgy could wind much faster because Lindy was holding the wool tight. Together they worked and chatted. Lindy told Cludgy all about her school in Brighton and then about the school in Portsmouth. She talked about Aunt Joan, and how she sorted her mother's beautiful clothes. A shudder went through Lindy at that moment. She pictured her mother in those clothes. They were quiet for a minute. Cludgy broke the silence and related stories from her school. She had gone to a Catholic convent school where the nuns were quite strict.

'I was never caned, although I was often threatened. However, the nuns threatened us with something more powerful. God! I was not quite sure what God was going to do to me and I am still waiting! At the time I was very frightened.'

They didn't realise just how long they had been

43

working until Arthur and Texi came in.

'Hello you two! Been busy?' he said.

Texi rushed up to Lindy expecting to be noticed. 'My hands are full, Texi, I'll stroke you later.'

'Nearly finished,' said Cludgy. 'We've got one more skein to do and then we're done. Then I'll get your supper.'

After they had eaten, Lindy went with Arthur to close up the hen house whilst Cludgy did the washing up. When they got back, Cludgy had started knitting. 'I'll have this done in no time,' she said, 'off you go to bed, pet.'

Lindy was too tired to overhear anything of the nine o'clock news. She was asleep as soon as her head hit the pillow.

On Thursday, Reggie called for Lindy and they walked to school together, Lindy in her makeshift uniform of brown coloured skirt, cream blouse and old green cardigan. She still looked smarter that Reggie who had dressed in his usual haphazard way. His shirt collar was half up, his tie was twisted, and his socks were around his ankles. He had slung his jumper over his shoulders. His shorts, which were straight as they were being held up by a pair of stout new braces, could be clearly seen.

'They're new!' said Reggie and he put his thumbs in the elastic straps and pulled them out and then let them go. 'Ow!' he screeched as they hit his chest.

Lindy half laughed, 'You're an idiot!'

'I know. Good isn't it? It made you laugh.'

The most notable event about that Thursday was Reggie's outburst of historical information in class. He told the class that Henry VIII had destroyed the local abbey.

'You can see the remains in the fields where the sheep graze,' he proudly announced. 'There's even a tree growing out of a broken window frame.'

His pride in himself was enhanced when Miss Simons said that he was quite correct. She then continued with the reasons why the abbeys were destroyed, and added in her talk the words, 'as Reggie so rightly said'. Reggie's smile went from ear to ear!

Lindy made a mental note to tell her father all about Reggie's special moment in the letter she was writing. She was looking forward to sending it. Her father had never written to her before, it was always her mother who wrote. He often wrote a sentence or two, but always signed them.

Reggie couldn't wait to get home that day.

'Oh, do hurry up Lindy, I want to get home! I want to tell Auntie Bee all about today.' Lindy hurried but could not keep up with Reggie: he was far too fast for her.

Lindy walked into the kitchen where the room was set up for ironing. The table had been moved towards the window. There was a folded blanket on it. An iron was plugged in to the overhead light. On the blanket there were pieces of navy-blue knitting.

'Hello, my pet!' she called to Lindy. 'Look! I've

finished knitting your jumper.'

On the grey blanket on the kitchen table were navy-blue knitted pieces. These were curled up at the edges. Cludgy pinned each piece in turn to the blanket gently pushing them out to their full shape. Then she took a wet, squeezed-out tea towel, placed it on top of the knitted pieces and gently pressed down with the hot iron.

'This is to get the pieces flat and ready to be sewn together.'

Absorbed in the process, Lindy and Cludgy failed to hear Arthur come in.

He looked very serious.

'I heard a whisper that they've got some of our lads off from Dunkirk.'

Cludgy stopped and looked at her husband.

'Dear God, help them!' she said.

6

The Blue Jumper

On Friday, Lindy came down fully dressed for breakfast. 'Morning Cludgy!' she said.

'Morning Lindy. You can take off the old green cardigan and put on your new navy-blue jumper.'

'Oh Cludgy! Did you stay up all night to sew it up?' asked Lindy.

'Well, no, not **all** night! It didn't take that long at all. Put it on, Lindy, put it on! I can't wait to see you in it.' Just who was more excited about the jumper, Cludgy or Lindy, was hard to tell.

'It's come out well,' said Cludgy. 'Go and look at yourself in the mirror, there's one on the wall in my bedroom. Run up and have a look. Arthur is out feeding the chickens.'

Lindy charged upstairs and along the corridor to the main bedroom. She squealed with delight! 'Oh Cludgy! It's beautiful, so smooth and neat. I'll look after it, I promise. Forever!'

Cludgy stood at the bottom of the stairs enjoying Lindy's reaction. 'I'm not sure about the "forever", I think you might grow out of it.'

'Oh, thank you, thank you,' Lindy gushed again and again. 'It's just perfect! Perfect. Just so perfect!'

Cludgy, who was becoming a little uncomfortable with all the praise, cleared her throat.

47

'Now' she said, 'let's get your breakfast. It's nearly time you left for school. Porridge alright for you today? Arthur's not back from the chickens.'

'Yes please.'

Lindy enjoyed her porridge. Cludgy had put the top of the milk on it and had added a spoonful of runny honey in the middle. She remembered porridge for breakfast at Oakleigh in Brighton. It was nothing like this. She remembered her friends there, and the brown and gold uniform, and wondered what they were doing.

'We had porridge a lot at my old school,' she said. 'It was not nearly as good at yours!'

'You've moved on now,' said Cludgy.

'Yes, nice porridge and a nice navy-blue jumper!' They both laughed at her silly joke.

Reggie knocked on the door. As soon as Lindy opened it, Reggie started chatting about smugglers on the beach. The children left for school, Reggie dressed as usual in short trousers, white shirt and blue jumper. His long grey socks were around his ankles already and his shoes were scuffed. Lindy, however, was smartly dressed in her new jumper and brown skirt. Her socks were pulled up and her shoes were cleaned.

Cludgy watched the friends walk up the lane.

'Chalk and cheese,' she muttered to herself. 'They couldn't be any more different! I'll have to do something about a navy-blue skirt for Lindy when I can get some material.'

48

Reggie did his usual run and stop on the journey, waiting for Lindy and calling out, 'Come on Slow Coach!' When she caught up with him, he continued with his stories about smugglers.

'I've got a new jumper!' Lindy proffered.

'Oh yeah, it's nice.'

Lindy told him the story of the bartering that Cludgy had done, and how she had made a jumper out of one of Arthur's.

At least Reggie was quiet as she spoke.

'Oh yeah it's nice,' he repeated, and then continued on about smugglers and the brandy they carried under the boats.

The jumper had the same reaction at school. No-one noticed. No-one said a word about it. It appeared that no-one cared.

There was one difference though. At playtime, some girls had managed to get a ball and were practising throwing it into the netball hoop. Lindy was invited to join in. How she had hated netball at Oakleigh in Brighton: she was never very good at it. But here she enjoyed it. She kept missing the net, again and again. Every time she tried, it went too far to the right and then the left or it was not high enough. But the girls weren't nasty or sneering; they called out, 'Shame!' and 'Nearly got it that time!' However, when she finally landed one in the net, they all cheered.

Lindy went back into class with a smile on her face.

49

At the end of the day, there was one person who did notice the new jumper. 'I like your new jumper,' Miss Simons called out as Lindy was packing up her books.

'Thank you,' Lindy said politely. 'Cludgy, I mean Mrs Sparrow, knitted it for me. We unpicked one of Mr Sparrow's jumpers and made this.'

'It has come out very well. She is a talented lady.'

'We're unpicking my old school jumper and the wool from that will go towards making a new jumper for Mr Sparrow.'

'That's a very good idea. I'm glad you're fitting in well here. This school must be so different from Oakleigh.'

'Oh yes, it is,' agreed Lindy. 'How did you know so much about my old schools?'

'Your father took great care to make sure you would be happy here and wrote me a letter explaining every detail about your previous schools. I gather the one in Portsmouth was not so good.'

'The teacher had a cane and kept hitting the desk with it when he spoke. He also caned some of the children too.' Lindy looked around the room, a little scared that she had said too much.

'Yes Lindy,' Miss Simons said pre-empting Lindy's thoughts. 'I do have a cane, but I rarely use it. I don't find it useful. I prefer to make the lesson as interesting as possible so there's no need to threaten anyone with the cane.'

Lindy smiled; she liked Miss Simons and felt

confident enough to ask suddenly, 'Where is Dunkirk? Why are the soldiers being brought home?'

'Dunkirk is in Northern France,' explained Miss Simons, 'and the Royal Navy is bringing our army home to England.'

'Why aren't they still fighting there?'

Miss Simons shivered at the thought of what was going on. 'Because the Germans have invaded France.' She felt that that was enough to tell a ten-year-old girl at that moment.

'Now you must get home to Mrs Sparrow. She's such a nice lady, don't you think? I've heard she's a good cook. An excellent cook in fact. I wonder what she has for your supper today? I'll see you on Monday.' She then paused, tidied her desk and added, 'Goodbye Lindy, have a nice weekend.'

'Yes, I must go, Reggie is waiting for me outside.'

As she got to the door she turned and called out 'Bye Miss!' *Then she remembered, she would have had to say 'Good evening or good night, Miss Simons' were she still at Oakleigh. Life is so much easier here.*

The walk home was filled with plans for the weekend. Reggie was going to show Lindy all the places where the smugglers used to land their contraband. They parted at Cludgy's door.

'I'll see you tomorrow,' said Reggie 'and then I can tell you all about the smugglers in Little Bridge.'

'What time?' called Lindy.

51

'Oh early, we've lots to see.' Reggie disappeared into his front door and was gone.

Early! thought Lindy, *whatever did that mean?*

7
The Letter

The house was quiet when Lindy woke on Saturday. The blackouts had been taken down and the sun shone through the gap in the curtains. A blackbird was perched on a branch of the climbing rose outside her window, singing to his heart's content.

Lindy stretched. 'Good morning Mr Blackbird,' she said.

She gently opened the curtains.

'Well, Mr Blackbird, it's a lovely day!'

He continued his song.

From her window, Lindy could see Arthur and Cludgy at the hen house across the lane. In front of them were the rows of vegetables and at the side an area of grass covered in buttercups and daisies. She saw Arthur put his arm around his wife's shoulder and give her a squeeze. Cludgy looked upset as she turned to look at her husband.

Suddenly Lindy was struck with a tinge of jealousy as she remembered how daddy used to cuddle mum. She always turned to look at him, and he always kissed her on the forehead. Cludgy pressed her face into Arthur's strong shoulders, and they paused there a moment. 'Look Mr Blackbird, my daddy used to hold my mummy like that.'

The blackbird continued singing. 'Aren't you paying attention to me at all, Mr Blackbird?' Lindy continued. 'Is there a Mrs Blackbird?' The blackbird flew off.

Lindy was dressed and coming downstairs when she overheard Arthur and Cludgy come into the kitchen.

'Those poor lads, they must be so frightened,' Cludgy said.

'I know, but the Royal Navy is over there picking them up as we speak. We have just got to hope ...'

'And pray,' interrupted Cludgy.

'And pray,' Arthur repeated, 'that they will be safely returned to England.'

Lindy walked in the door. 'Good morning, Lindy my dear. What a fine day it's going to be,' announced Arthur.

'Morning pet' joined in Cludgy. 'The hens have laid today. I can spare at least one egg each this morning, but I'm hoping to swap some eggs for some margarine with Doris, who lives at number 10. I don't know where she gets it from, but I don't ask. Shall I boil the eggs for you both?'

'Thank you,' said Lindy.

'That would be lovely,' said Arthur.

Arthur and Lindy laid the table. Three slices of thick bread were put under the grill for toasting and the eggs were carefully put in the saucepan of boiling water.

'Arthur, would you time four and a half minutes for the eggs, please?' asked Cludgy.

'Shall I watch the toast?' offered Lindy.

Before Cludgy could answer, they spotted the postman outside the door. 'Just the one today,' he called out. 'It's for a Miss Lindy Elliot.'

'Ooo … that's for you my dear,' said Cludgy 'I wonder who it's from. Leave the toast, I'll do that. You read your letter.'

Getting letters was a joy beyond anything for Lindy. She remembered the long letters from her mum when she was at school in Brighton. She recalled how she liked to find a quiet spot on her own where she could read them and enjoy every word.

'It's from my Daddy. He has written so soon. I've a half-written letter to him. I must finish that one and send it to him.'

She felt it would be a little rude if she left the room to be alone to read it, so she carefully opened up the precious envelope at the table. There were two pages and a strip of six stamps. Lindy stared and stared at the contents. There were not a lot of words to read but a lot of drawings of pin men. There were pin men climbing ladders, one holding a hose with lots of water pouring out. Lots of pin men were running about all over the paper.

The paper was folded in two, and across the fold there were two drawings of beaches, one on the left-hand side of the page and one on the opposite. In between the two drawings, there were waves and fishes, as in the sea. On each beach was a pin man. On the right-hand side of the paper there was a large one with a helmet on, whilst on the left-hand side there was a smaller one in a skirt. They were waving at each other and blowing kisses. The

55

kisses (marked liked X's) were flying over the sea from left to right and from right to left.

'What does he say?' asked Arthur.

'He doesn't say much. He hopes I'm well and settled in here with you. He hopes I'm enjoying my new school. He sends his regards to you both and wishes you well too. That's all really.'

'But there are two pages!' exclaimed Arthur.

'I know! It's full of drawings. Look!' She showed them the pages and explained, 'Dad was never one for writing long letters.'

'Well, well! That is one way to avoid any trouble with the censors who may pick it up. It's like a code.' Arthur said.

'What fun!' said Cludgy.

Together they worked out what the pin men were doing in each drawing, which were mostly showing what he did in his training as a fireman. All of a sudden Lindy squealed, as she understood the illustration of the two beaches. 'Oh! I get it!' she exclaimed. 'That's Daddy and that's me! We're sending kisses to each other. Where is the beach from here? I want to go there and blow kisses!'

'Apparently, Reggie is going to take you on an expedition this morning and I think he's planned a visit to the beach. He told Betsy and she told me,' said Cludgy.

Despite the disruption of the letter the toast did not burn and the eggs were just right.

'When you go to the beach, you must not go into the

water.' Arthur spoke seriously, 'I'll take you there for a swim one day, I promise, but on your own you must stay on the sand.'

'Of course, I promise,' said Lindy.

Lindy couldn't wait to tell Reggie about her letter. 'It's full of drawings of himself at work.' In fact, she couldn't think nor talk about anything else.

'I'm going to show you a famous grave,' Reggie said as he opened the gate to the church yard. There was a carving above the gate. Referring to it he said, 'I was told what it was called, but I've forgotten … but it's old, very old.' He found the gravestone very quickly.

'There!' he said. 'It's the gravestone marking the place of the smuggler. They say he was an innocent man who was shot. However,' and Reggie looked earnestly at Lindy and lowered his voice, 'there's a story that he was guilty and that he was smuggling!'

Lindy did not react to his dramatic story, as she was too absorbed in her own thoughts. In fact, she wasn't listening at all. 'When are we going to the beach?' she asked.

'That's the orchard, where you get apples from,' Reggie announced, pointing to the apple trees behind the hedge opposite the church. 'Jolly nice they are too.' Lindy stretched her neck to look.

'I got lots of apples from there last September when I came.'

'Didn't they mind that you took their apples?' Lindy

asked.

'Don't know, didn't ask.' Reggie shrugged his shoulders.

'Isn't that stealing?' continued Lindy. 'How did you get in?'

'Through the hedge. There's a hole further up the road. Anyway, it's not stealing.'

'What? It is too!' Lindy was shouting now.

'It was harvest time in church and we sang "All good gifts around us are sent from heaven above" so I thought God wouldn't mind, so I crawled through the hedge and took a couple. Well, to be truthful, I took a few. They were nice.'

'Nice or not, they belonged to someone else, not you!'

'Well, I never got caught, so obviously God didn't mind.'

Lindy was glad that it was spring and that there were no apples left on the trees for him to demonstrate how he took them.

'I cut my knee quite badly on one trip!' said Reggie proudly.

'How many times did you take the apples?'

'A few!' said Reggie. By now he realised that Lindy was getting a little cross, and he wisely thought he shouldn't talk about it anymore. 'Let's go to the beach!'

Reggie led her back through the old gate with the funny face on top and back past the cottages and down a very steep hill.

At the bottom there was a stream, which ran under the road. 'This is the actual Little Bridge,' announced Reggie.

'It's very little. Did they really name a village after a bridge this small?' questioned Lindy.

'It was only a small village when it was named. I suppose it's grown now.'

There was a wide path in front of them with large paving stones on one side. A brook followed the line of stones. It widened as it opened out on to the beach. Together in single file they followed it to the end. The golf course was on the right and there were woods on the left. There were two houses hidden in the woods with lots of farm animals in a clearing in front. Reggie announced that there were small fishing boats stored on the beach.

'Mr Sparrow fishes from this beach and sometimes goes out on a boat. I don't think he owns one though.'

As the sea came into view, Lindy fastened her pace. 'Hurry up Reggie!' she said, 'I want to see the sea and Portsmouth.'

8
Golf Balls

Lindy ran towards the shore. The water was very still. She looked straight across to the mainland.

'Portsmouth is over there, past the pier,' shouted Reggie, pointing to the right.

It was so far away, she thought. She sat down on a rock and just stared across the water. Shutting her eyes, she pictured her daddy, dressed in his smart suit that he used to wear to work at the department store. Then she thought of the photo that she had taken of him cuddling up with her mother on the beach. She allowed herself a short smile, but her eyes became wet and so she opened them and gazed out to sea.

'You've got to be careful,' she said out loud, as if to her father, 'and come back to me.'

She was so deep in her thoughts that she didn't see Reggie disappear. The sea was calm, the sun was shining, it was so beautiful.

'If there wasn't a war and I hadn't been evacuated and had to be living away from my father,' she said to Reggie, 'then all this would be just wonderful, wouldn't it?'

There was no reply, as Reggie was not there. She drew her knees up, wrapped her arms around her lower legs and cuddled them unaware that Reggie wasn't there or that he didn't reply.

All of a sudden, he reappeared from a hole in the hedge. There was an extra mud stain on his already dirty shirt. He rubbed it to try and remove the mark.

'No luck!' he said. 'Perhaps it'll come out in the wash.'

'Where have you been?' asked Lindy.

'On the golf course,' he said with a wide grin. 'Look, I've managed to find three golf balls.' He passed one to Lindy.

'It's as hard as a stone,' she remarked.

She handed it back and he stuffed them in his pocket.

'They may have been part of a game, and you've taken them. They won't be able to play anymore without their golf balls.'

'Nah, you have to be rich to belong to the golf club. They've got plenty. They can get another one out of their bag.'

'But,' Lindy protested, 'the game is that you hit the ball with a club around the course, from the start to the hole using the same ball. They count the shots as they go. The winner is the one who does the course in the least number of shots.'

'Silly game if you ask me. What happens if they lose their ball?'

'They have to add a shot to their score. Oh Reggie, you're not being very nice, are you?'

Reggie shrugged his shoulders.

The bay was quite small. There was not a lot to see.

61

They walked to the end towards the pier, and then as far as they could the other way, carefully jumping over the stream that they had followed down the path. There was a big pond behind a wall. Lindy could just about see over it; Reggie could not until he climbed up to have a look.

'You've scuffed your shoes now!' scolded Lindy.

They wandered back towards the path. Lindy's jump over the stream was not so successful this time and she landed in the water, drenching her shoes.

'Ugh, I've got my socks wet too! It feels horrid. I'll take them off and go home with just my shoes on.'

She sat down, took off her shoes and removed her soggy socks. She squeezed them out as much as she could and shoved them down into the pocket of her dress. Unfortunately, her clean hanky was in there, as her mother had taught her. It was essential that she had a clean hanky on her. 'Now my hanky is wet too,' she wailed.

'Hey Lindy, just a minute. Look!' said Reggie. 'There are no boats! They can't all be out fishing. Can they?'

'It is Saturday after all, maybe they are,' said Lindy, doing up the buckles on her sandals. 'Let's go home now. My feet are really uncomfortable.'

Arthur, who had Texi on a lead, was coming from the field opposite the cottage when they walked up the lane. 'Hello you two, where have you been?'

Texi greeted Lindy and Reggie in his usual manner. Wagging his tail, he jumped up first on Lindy and then on

Reggie. They both stooped down and made a fuss of him.

'Just to the beach,' said Reggie. 'Lindy wanted to see Portsmouth. Can't think why, you can't see much of it anyway.'

Arthur knew. 'Time for lunch!' he said.

After finding clean, dry socks Lindy sat down with Cludgy and Arthur for a salad sandwich lunch.

'Whilst you two were paddling,' said Cludgy, 'I have had a very successful morning. As I walked through our allotment, I discovered two ripe tomatoes. I thought they would be nice in a cheese and tomato sandwich, then I remembered we've no cheese at the moment.'

She cut each sandwich into two pieces, carefully presented them on plates and laid them on the table.

Arthur picked up his plate, held it in line with his eyes and examined his lunch. 'I thought that green was a funny looking cheese,' he said

'Oh Arthur, I'm coming to that!' Cludgy raised her eyes and looked at Lindy. 'Then I found some early lettuce leaves that I could take from a couple of plants.'

'Oh I see!' said Arthur. 'It's not cheese then?'

Lindy and Cludgy sighed.

'I also managed to get Texi a bone from the butcher,' continued Cludgy. 'I was lucky it is very difficult to get any meat for dogs at the moment.'

Texi sat in his basket happily gnawing at it.

'Don't go near him at the moment,' warned Arthur. 'He won't like it if someone gets too close.' As if to make

63

his point Texi growled aggressively.

'Best leave him on his own until he has finished it,' Cludgy said.

Lindy told them where they had been and asked about the golf club. 'Are you a member, Arthur?' asked Lindy.

'No... no ... you have to be someone to belong there, and have lots of money too,' he replied. 'Anyway, I prefer to do other things rather than chase a small ball around a course. It seems to me that it's just a long walk ruined by having to hit the ball with a long stick.'

'Arthur, I'm sure they get a lot of pleasure out of hitting a small ball and walking around a course,' Cludgy said.

'Apparently there's a search light battery sited on the course. I hope nobody hits the light with a golf ball. They might smash it and the light would go out. Those balls are quite hard.'

'Yes, I know,' said Lindy.

'How do you know? Have you played?'

'No, no. A friend at my school in Brighton, ... her parents played and ... she brought a ball into school.' Lindy was lying but thought better of telling them that Reggie had managed to get three of them in his pocket today. Quickly she managed to change the subject. 'There were no boats on the shore. Reggie said that there are usually lots. Where will they be? Are they all out fishing, do you think?'

'Quite possibly!' said Arthur. It was now his turn to change the subject. He was sure that the fishing boats were being used across the channel helping to get British soldiers out from Dunkirk. 'Have we got a pudding today, Cludgy?'

'Well! I've been able to make a cake today. I swapped some eggs for some flour and butter. I didn't have quite enough fat, so I added some dripping, only a little, mind. So, I hope you can't taste it. I was saving the cake for tea, but shall we have a slice now?'

Cludgy's cake was delicious.

'I can't taste the dripping in it,' announced Arthur, 'can you Lindy?'

'No, not at all! The jam in the middle is lovely.'

'Ah, now, my clever wife made the jam too!' continued Arthur. 'We had a really good crop of raspberries last summer and Cludgy made jam from it. We also have plum jam and just a few pots of strawberry.'

'There would have been more, but Arthur kept pinching the fruit.'

Arthur put on a guilty face, which made Lindy and Cludgy laugh.

'By the way, I heard as I was cleaning the church with Betsy this morning that the police were called to the golf club!' remarked Cludgy.

'Whatever for?' said Arthur.

'A very serious crime!' she teased them further. 'So serious that the superintendent of police is involved.'

'What crime?' Lindy asked.

Cludgy put on a stern sober face. 'Theft!' she said dramatically.

'What on earth has been stolen?' asked Arthur.

'Golf balls!'

Lindy shuddered.

9
Remorse

Needless to say, Lindy was desperate to go and find Reggie. She had lied to Arthur and Cludgy. She knew something about the theft and that made her guilty. Finishing her cake as quickly as she could, she wiped her mouth with her serviette, folded it, and put it back into the serviette ring.

Arthur leaned back in his chair, 'Thank you my dear wife for a delicious lunch. The sandwiches were excellent, the pudding superb and the service tremendous.'

'Oh stop it!' said Cludgy. 'You're embarrassing me.'

'Yes, thank you. I did enjoy it,' said Lindy hurriedly, 'especially the cake.'

'There will be more at teatime.'

'Shall I help you with the clearing up Cludgy, before I go out to play?' asked Lindy.

'There's so very little to clear away, you get along now and enjoy the fine weather.'

Without even saying goodbye to Texi, Lindy ran next door and knocked for Reggie. Still with his mouth full, Reggie came to the door.

'Hurry up, I need to talk to you!' Lindy said. 'NOW!'

She led the way into the churchyard and found a spot behind some gravestones. 'Listen Reggie, listen very carefully. We're going to be in serious trouble!'

'Why?'

67

'The golf balls!' Lindy shouted. 'The police have been called!'

'What? They're only golf balls. There are loads of them.'

'Yes! And you've got some of them! Just how many have you got?'

'Well, I don't rightly know. I've been collecting them since last September when I arrived. There was no one to play with, so I sneaked around the golf course. I wasn't seen; that was the whole point.'

'I suppose you thought you were a soldier on a secret mission or something,' suggested Lindy.

'It was fun! I've got about a bucket full.'

'Where are they?' asked Lindy

'Here,' said Reggie, 'in the graveyard, well hidden. Well, no one has found them yet! They're behind a tree in a corner over there.'

Sure enough, between the tree and the wall there was a bucket, well hidden, covered over with newspaper, a sack and the ivy.

'I had to cover them as the bucket filled with water in the winter. They would be no good for selling if they were damaged.'

'SELLING THEM!' shrieked Lindy. 'Who on earth do you think would buy these stolen golf balls?'

Reggie shrugged his shoulders! 'Don't know really,' he said, 'there's a golf club up the road.'

'And you got the balls from that golf club!'

The children sat down on the grass leaning against the tomb stone of Thomas Smith, who died in 1793. Lindy was contemplating just what trouble they were in.

'Are we going to get caught?' whispered Reggie.

'Quite possibly if we can't find a way of getting rid of this bucket full of golf balls! Just how do you think we're going to get out of this mess?' Lindy said.

They paused for a moment.

'We could take them back,' suggested Reggie breaking the silence.

'Are you suggesting we go up to the clubhouse door and hand them in!'

'No, we could leave them around the place. The course is enormous. We could sort of scatter them. One ball looks much like another. Some players may think they've done better than they thought!'

'Or worse!' Lindy thought for a moment. 'That's not such a bad idea. The first place we'll start at is where you got the last ones this morning.'

'Brilliant! Let's get started' shouted Reggie, rushing towards the bucket.

'Wait a minute!'

'What?'

'How are we going to carry all those balls, we can't go wandering along carrying the bucket, we'll be sure to be spotted.'

'Pockets!' Reggie suggested

Even with the children's pockets stuffed full, there

was still half a bucket left. They sat down and thought.

'What about our gas mask boxes?' suggested Lindy. 'No-one would know what was in them, they'd assume they're gas masks. We'll have to sneak back home to get them.'

'Mine's hanging up near the front door,' said Reggie. 'Won't be difficult to get in without being seen.'

'With our pockets and the gas mask boxes full, it still won't be enough.' The children sat down again quietly and pondered.

Suddenly Reggie shouted, 'A picnic!' He was full of ideas.

Lindy was furious! 'How can you think about more food at this time? You've just had dinner. Here I am trying to think of ways of getting us out of trouble. Trouble that's **all** down to you. Really!' Lindy was red in the face and was getting more and more angry.

'No, Lindy! Listen!'

'Alright, I'm listening!' she snapped.

'We could **pretend** that we're going for a picnic and carry a bag. You've got a school bag, haven't you? Instead of sandwiches in the bag we'll put the golf balls.'

Lindy thought for a while, 'Yes, yes,' she said, 'I think that would work. Not a bad idea, Reggie! Not a bad idea at all.'

She rushed back to the cottage, where she found Cludgy washing up. 'Hello, did you forget something?'

'No ... err ... yes ... err I need to go to the lavatory.'

70

Lindy felt uncomfortable as she was lying again! She found her bag and her gas mask box hanging up near the lavatory door. She pulled the lavatory chain to carry on the deception. Then she stuffed the bags under her dress and rushed through the kitchen. There was no need to worry. Cludgy wasn't there.

Back in the churchyard, they took out their gas masks and hid them behind the tree.

'Horrid things,' commented Lindy.

Then they emptied the remainder of the bucket of balls into the empty gas mask boxes and Lindy's school satchel. Lindy carried this on her back.

With bulging pockets and a heavy bag of golf balls, the children slung their gas mask boxes over their shoulders and set off down the steep hill to Little Bridge and along to the beach. When the coast was clear Reggie crawled through the hedge again and threw three balls around the area. He was close to the hole so he popped an extra one in.

Reggie crawled back through the gap, and they returned to the lane and started up the hill towards the golf club. Some golfers were walking across the lane carrying their bags. Suddenly Reggie scrabbled about in the hedge.

'Here Mister!' he shouted. 'Look what I found in the hedge.'

The golfer was tall and dressed up in big baggy trousers, which were held tight at the lower leg. 'Yes, what is it?' he said rather haughtily.

'Look what I found sir.' Reggie held up the golf ball in his thumb and first finger. 'It's a golf ball ain't it?'

The golfer looked down on Reggie, which made him feel smaller than ever.

'It's what you play with, ain't it?' Reggie continued.

'Of course it is, boy!' the large man said with such self-importance.

'Do you want it?' asked Reggie.

'Not really. I have more than enough but I'll take it.'

'Here you are then,' said Reggie handing it over.

'Thank you, young man!' the golfer said.

Lindy was relieved, as she was not sure what Reggie would have said if the golfer hadn't said thank you.

'I say! By the way,' the golfer continued trying to be friendly. 'What is in your satchel?'

'Our picnic!' lied Reggie.

'A picnic! I hope you're not planning to eat the contents of that bag on any part of the golf course. We certainly don't want you ruining our greens and fairways.'

The response to this was easy. The children happily said, 'No sir.'

Then Lindy added 'Of course not, sir. We wouldn't dream of it!'

'Well! That's alright then!' said the golfer. 'Nice to see you have your gas masks with you. You never know what the enemy will do.'

The friends stood together and smiled sweetly. Reggie leaned over to Lindy and whispered 'They didn't have their gas masks with them.'

'We don't have our gas masks with us either.' she whispered back. 'Come on let's get moving.'

Reggie and Lindy continued on their journey. They threw balls over the hedge and sometimes when the area was empty with no one around, Reggie crawled under the hedge and along the ground. He buried a few in various bunkers brushing over the area with his hand so that they were really hidden. Some were left in long grass. Reggie even tried to get one fixed in a tree. He failed. Lindy had to drag him away. They walked down, then up the long driveway of Channel House, and chucked a few over the fence.

They ended up on Ladies Lane near the clubhouse. Looking through the hedge, Reggie spotted the ideal place to get rid of a few more. Up against the wall next to the clubhouse door were six golf bags. They were standing there, their tops open just ready to receive a golf ball. Reggie looked all around the car park. It was deserted. He took his chance, slipped through the gate and darted over the open ground to the door. He put his back flat against the wall and caught his breath. When he was sure it was clear he put at least one ball in each bag. Again, he waited, until he was sure he had not been spotted, then he ran back to the gate which Lindy was holding open for him. Safely behind the hedge, they sat on the ground and giggled.

'What will they think when they empty their bags out and find an extra ball?' said Lindy in a low voice.

Through his giggles, Reggie managed to add, 'I put two in some!'

Their laughing was abruptly curtailed as they spotted a policeman arriving on his bike. He propped this against the hedge close to the friends. Reggie and Lindy held their breath and didn't move. The policeman took off his bicycle clips and put them in his pocket. He shook out his trousers by stamping his feet. He then brushed down his jacket with his hands and looked down to check his trousers again. He looked as though he was going to enter somewhere very important and must look the part. Out of the corner of his eye, he spotted a bright white golf ball on the ground. It was lying close to the children. They gasped and put their hands over their mouths. They were sure to be spotted now. He picked up the ball, looked around, put the ball in his pocket and then walked towards the clubhouse.

'Phew! I thought we were nearly for it then,' gasped Lindy.

Reggie was quiet and then he said, 'Hey Lindy!' He paused. 'Look!' He paused again. 'How many balls have we got left?'

'Just a few!'

'I've got an idea to get rid of those. Give them to me.'

Reggie had spotted that the policeman's bike had a saddlebag. Before Lindy could stop him, he slipped through the gate again and approached the bike. He quickly unbuckled the bag's cover and carefully and quietly slipped in the last of the golf balls. Lindy's heart was thumping, she was feeling slightly sick. She was sure that someone would spot him. Her anguish was prolonged as he replaced the cover and did the buckle up again before he crept back through the gate.

Free from golf balls the children ran back down the

lane. They didn't stop running until they reached the bridge. They walked down to the beach and laid down on the sand.

Reggie was very proud of himself. Not only had he pinched, undetected, a large quantity of golf balls, but he had successfully given them back, equally without being caught.

Lindy was feeling a mixture of pride and relief. Pride that they had managed to get rid of all the balls, and relief that they weren't caught as she didn't want her father to know what a naughty thing she had been involved in.

On the way back to the churchyard to retrieve their gas masks Reggie pondered, 'I wonder what will happen when the balls are discovered in the policeman's saddle bag.'

'I've heard that they share their bikes,' replied Lindy.

'Will people think that the policeman was the golf ball thief?'

10
The Other Beach

Lindy was used to going to church. It was a ritual that she was involved in at school. The church was next door to the cottage. It was a pretty little place with a feeling of friendliness. Lindy could not remember all the people she was introduced to, but they were all very welcoming and nice.

Auntie Bee was there with Reggie, whose experience of going to church had been limited. He had attended every Sunday since September 1939 when he first arrived.

The hymns they sang were familiar to Lindy. There were prayers for the soldiers in France. She didn't quite understand all of the sermon but the vicar spoke in such a lovely soft voice, it really didn't matter what he said. He said it very nicely.

Whilst Cludgy was getting dinner, Arthur busied himself in the vegetable patch. Lindy sat at the kitchen table and continued her letter to her father. She was deeply involved in her writing, only asking Cludgy for the odd spelling. Her new jumper figured prominently and how it was created. It was a little difficult to know what else to write, as everything that had happened with Reggie referred back to the golf balls and she couldn't tell him about that.

After lunch Lindy finished four pages of her letter to her daddy. She addressed the envelope and carefully stuck on one of the stamps he had sent her.

Reggie knocked for Lindy. 'Want to come out and play, Lindy?'

'May I, Cludgy?

Cludgy remembered her childhood towards the end of the last century. She had not been allowed to go out and play on Sundays. She had to stay at home and read, preferably a religious book or the bible. However, the world was so different now, they were at war. Who knew what would happen in the future? It was all so unsettling. 'Of course you can, go and enjoy yourselves.' she said.

'Thanks,' Lindy and Reggie said in unison. 'Oh, my letter!' said Lindy, 'I must post that first.'

Lindy and Reggie walked around to the post box. The route was well away from the golf course. Lindy thought it prudent that they go nowhere near the place for the time being. She shivered every time she thought about those golf balls.

They walked around Little Bridge. They found two swings at the top of the road near the school on the corner of a field. Ever competitive, Reggie challenged Lindy to see who could go the highest. She let him win every time, not liking the feeling of being that far off the ground.

Their route around the village took them near some woods, not far from the church. There was a notice displayed. It said "Bird Sanctuary. Entry prohibited."

Lindy read the notice out loud.

78

'What does probehibitited mean?' asked Reggie.

'I don't really know, but I think it means that we shouldn't go in.'

'Well **I** don't know what probehibitited means, and **you're** not sure, so it doesn't mean us. Let's go in.'

They followed a well-worn single-track path. It was densely covered with ivy, hazelnut trees and large amounts of brambles.

'Ouch!' said Lindy. 'I've been scratched.'

'Oh, it's nothing. It's only a bramble,' said Reggie, as he carelessly turned around and scratched his leg too. He already had a fine collection of bumps, bruises and scabs on his legs. 'One more won't make any difference,' he bragged.

'Shush!' said Lindy in a low voice. 'Can you hear that?'

'Hear what?' he replied.

'Voices. They're coming from over there,' said Lindy.

'Let's go and investigate. Quietly now, they may be robbers or German spies,' said Reggie, always looking for an adventure.

They lowered their stance and crept further towards the voices.

'Funny German spies, eh? They're shouting! And in perfect English,' said Lindy, 'with local accents.'

They came to a clearing. In the middle of it was a box and on that was seated Trevor from school, his hands covering his eyes. In front of him was a slope, which was the remains of an old quarry. He was counting out loud. 'Ninety-nine, one hundred. Coming! Ready or not!'

'That was never a hundred!' said an unseen voice.

'Was too!' Trevor replied.

Trevor, now standing, looked around him and walked down the hill towards the unseen voice. 'Found you, Mary, I knew it was your voice.'

'That was never one hundred!' she said. 'You can't count up to one hundred.'

'I can too!' he snarled back.

Just then their argument ceased as they spotted Lindy and Reggie.

'Hey, what are you doing here?' said Trevor.

'This is our spot!' said Mary. 'Nobody comes here except us.'

'We just found it,' argued Lindy. 'You were easy to find, you were making so much noise.'

'AND!'... announced Reggie, as he wandered down the slope, 'there's a notice to say that entry is probehibitited! You shouldn't be here anyway!'

Just then there was a shout from the top of a tree nearby. 'Got you!' and two boys jumped down kicking the box, now vacated by Trevor, down the hill. It landed at Reggie's feet. He picked it up.

'Can we play?' Reggie asked.

Astounded by his cheek, there was silence. No-one spoke, as they all looked at each other.

'Well, I suppose so,' said a boy at the top of the hill,

'but I'm not sure about the girl!'

Reggie stood there holding the box like a trophy. 'If you don't let her play, then I'll tear up your box!'

'Oh OK then, she can play. Everyone agree?'

There was a mumble of agreement from the other three children. Mary, also from school, was especially glad as she was the only girl, and had been allowed in the game because her brother Henry was in the group. He had been told by his mother that he had to look after his younger sister. He was a large lad, two years older than the rest of the group, who were all in the same class at school. Henry had designated himself as the gang leader. His sidekick, also standing at the top of the hill, was Tony. He was half the size of Henry but thought him wonderful. Everything Henry said, Tony agreed.

'What's the game then?' asked Reggie.

'Kick the Can,' Henry said.

'Where's the can?' said Reggie.

'Gone to salvage, so we're using this old cardboard box instead.'

They took it in turns to be 'It', and they played for quite a while. Lindy and Mary slipped away and enjoyed a quite chat together. The game eventually came to an abrupt halt, when the box finally was deemed to be so broken that it could no longer take the part of being 'the can'.

Henry held the broken box and announced 'I'm hungry anyway! I'm going home.' Tony was the first to agree and then Trevor followed. Mary did not want to leave her new friend, but Henry was her brother, so she agreed.

'What shall we do Reggie?' Lindy asked her true friend.

'I know, I'll take you to the other beach,' said Reggie.

Together they retraced their steps, passed the sign prohibiting their entry, and walked down the road to a footpath.

The path was quite muddy to start with. Reggie showed Lindy how to walk on the small bank at the side. There were lots of beach cobbles to negotiate. 'Walk on them as if they're steppingstones in a stream,' instructed Reggie. 'It's easier that way.'

The path seemed to go on forever; Lindy was getting fed up with the route that was sometimes muddy and sometimes covered with stones. 'How much longer?' she asked.

'Not far, we'll get to the stinky bit and then you'll see the beach.'

'Stinky bit?'

'There's a bog at the end of the path and it stinks!'

It was true, Lindy smelt the bog before she saw it. 'Eugh!' she said, but then she looked up and there in front of her was an oak tree. The well-beaten path went both sides of it onto a sandy beach. The tide was in, and it was idyllic.

'Oh isn't this lovely?' she said.

82

There were a few people left on the sands and some were still bathing, but most people were leaving. 'It must be getting late,' said Lindy. 'We must go home.'

Ever ready for an adventure, Reggie suggested, 'We could go along the shoreline and find our way to the other beach where the fishing boats are.'

'Have you ever done that walk before?' asked Lindy

'No, but surely it must come out at the other beach.'

'The tide is high, we don't know if there's enough dry beach to walk on,' Lindy argued. 'Let's just go back the way we came.'

Reluctantly Reggie turned around and walked back along the sandy beach to the exit near the oak tree.

'We'll explore this another day,' said Lindy.

11
The War Gets Nearer

That evening Arthur, Cludgy and Lindy listened to the radio. Leading up to the news, Sandy MacPherson played the organ. Arthur relaxed in his chair, Texi at his side. Cludgy was knitting. She had nearly finished all the pieces of Arthur's jumper that were made out of Lindy's brown school jumper and left-over navy-blue wool.

'Do you like the navy trimmings around the neck and sleeves?' Cludgy asked.

'Yes, they're lovely,' said Lindy.

'Yes, I thought so too,' added Cludgy, 'quite smart. Arthur?'

'Yes dear?'

'Do you like the two colours in your new jumper?'

'Yes dear, lovely,' he replied. 'Sorry, I was miles away.'

Lindy too was sitting quietly deep in her own thoughts. With a strong sense of what was right and wrong, she worried about her part in yesterday's adventure. She concluded that she didn't steal them in the first place, but she was part of the 'doing the right thing', by returning the balls to the club.

Lindy was in bed well before Cludgy and Arthur listened to the rather grim news from Dunkirk on the nine o'clock news.

At school the next day, Miss Simons gave Lindy some

more challenging work, which she loved.

'Thank you, Miss Simons,' she gushed, 'thank you so much'.

'You'd think I'd given her a ten-bob note, not some schoolwork,' she told her colleagues at break time.

Lindy loved her new work, and that evening she spent completing the challenges that Miss Simons had set her. She had also lent her the book 'Pollyanna' by Eleanor Porter. Once Lindy had started to read the first chapter, she couldn't put it down. However, the smell of Cludgy's cooking enticed her away.

The book was the reason she did not go out to play on Tuesday. Once she had done her chores for Cludgy and read a chapter there was no time left for Reggie.

'You're getting boring, Lindy,' he said to her.

'Sorry, I'm too busy.'

On Wednesday, Lindy arrived home from school to find Cludgy at the sink preparing vegetables and Arthur at the dinner table, with a newspaper flat in front of him avidly reading.

'Hello Arthur!' Lindy called out.

Texi barked and bounced up on her which prompted Lindy to kneel down.

'Hello Texi, have you had a nice day?' she said as she ruffled his back and stroked his head. He continued to bark. Arthur however did not react. He remained still, totally mesmerised with what he was reading, almost unaware of Lindy and Texi in the room.

'Quiet Texi, Arthur is reading. Maybe I'll find time to take you for a walk.' Lindy said.

She moved closer and looked over Arthur's shoulder and read:

'335,000 MEN EVACUATED'

Underneath the headline was a large picture of men queuing up in the sea and on the beach. The subtitle said:

'Dunkirk at Last Abandoned:
The Withdrawal Complete'

Lindy was suddenly terrified. 'What does that mean?' she said. 'Have we lost the war?'

Arthur sprang to life and turned around. He took hold of her hands.

'No, no, my dear one,' he said. 'We have just lost this little bit of it.'

'It was miraculous that we managed to get all those lads out of France,' Cludgy added.

'There were lots of little private boats from all over the south of England which helped, including some of the fishing boats from Little Bridge. Things are going to get busy now. There will be no more talk of it being a "Phoney War".

Cludgy put her arms around Lindy. 'Don't fret now pet, we're going to be safe.'

'We've got Winston Churchill as our leader,' said Arthur.

'Oh yes, we can't fail with him as prime minister,' Cludgy added.

'I would imagine that we'll be making use of that Anderson Shelter we have in the walled garden,' Arthur continued.

'I'll get an emergency basket ready for us to pick up as soon as we hear the warning.'

'Do you mean that the Germans will bomb us now?' Lindy looked frightened.

'I'm not sure they will be interested in Little Bridge,' said Arthur.

Lindy thought of her father. She imagined him fighting the fires caused by the Germans. She saw him digging in the rubble looking for people in broken houses bombed by the Germans. Although only six years old at the time, in 1937 she had seen photos in the paper of the bombing of Guernica in Spain. She remembered the damaged houses, and people trying to dig in the rubble.

Cludgy saw Lindy's worried face. She pondered as to what to say and do for her charge.

'We have to carry on, Lindy, we have to be brave and get on with life the best way we can. Arthur and I will keep you as safe as we possibly can.'

'Yes, I know. Thank you Cludgy.'

'Now we must get our bits and pieces ready for the Anderson Shelter. Will you help me please?'

This gave the two of them something to do. After reading the paper, Arthur passed it on to Betsy's husband, Robert next door. He, in turn, handed Arthur a copy of the Daily Mirror.

'You need to read the front page,' he said.

He hadn't got back in the house for long when Reggie knocked. Even before Lindy had opened the door he blurted out, 'Are you coming down to the beach with me? I want to see the boats. Do you think they've bullet holes in them? Or perhaps they may have traces of blood!'

'Not now Reggie,' Lindy said quietly, aware of their shock at the photo and the news. 'Maybe tomorrow after school. Anyway, the boats aren't likely to be back so soon. They've only just finished sailing from France.' Reggie left.

Arthur returned to his seat at the table, opened the Daily Mirror and laid it flat. Cludgy and Lindy sat down quietly as Arthur began to read out loud Churchill's address to the nation.

'We shall fight in France, we shall fight on the seas and oceans, we shall fight with growing confidence and growing strength in the air, we shall defend our island, whatever the cost may be. We shall fight on the beaches, we shall fight on the landing grounds, we shall fight in the fields and in the streets, we shall fight in the hills; we shall never surrender.'

Cludgy jumped up. 'I'll fight them on the beaches,' she stated, 'No-one will get past me. Arthur! Will you teach me how to shoot a gun?'

'Gosh Cludgy, could you really kill a German?' asked Lindy.

'If any German tried to hurt you or Arthur, you bet I

could!' Cludgy spoke decisively. 'Or Texi, or Reggie for that matter.'

Arthur didn't reply.

Sleep was difficult that night. Arthur thought about the extra training he would have to do to prepare in case of invasion. Cludgy was worried about how she would get enough food to feed everyone. Lindy thought of her daddy and, for the first time since her arrival, she felt homesick and wanted to be with him, hold on to him tightly and never let him go.

The next day was a school day. At home-time Reggie and Lindy went straight to the beach, and looked at the boats. To Reggie's excitement, there were a couple of bullet holes, but no blood. Sadly, one of the boats was missing. There was no one who could explain why, nor what happened to the boat or its skipper. Unlike Reggie, Lindy really didn't want to know.

For the following few months, the teachers tried hard to keep a sense of normality. School started at nine o'clock if there had been no air raid warning, but ten o'clock if there had been. Lessons were a bit haphazard, as it was difficult for the teachers to prepare for lessons when they had to go to their shelters as soon as the air raid siren sounded.

Cludgy and Arthur tried to keep life as normal as possible. The air raids began, and they were frequent. By the middle of July there had been 25 air raid warnings. They hardly slept a night in the house. Most nights were spent in the air raid shelter.

Lindy was quite versed as what to do when the warning was heard. How she hated that whining noise. When it started, she got out of bed, put on her shoes, her dressing gown and quickly walked downstairs to the back door. Cludgy was waiting with her basket of essentials. Early in the evening she had made a Thermos of boiling water, so they could have a cup of freshly made tea in the shelter. She had the tea caddy in her basket together with the milk. Lindy had learnt to enjoy tea without sugar so there was no need to take it. At the start of the air raids, they had carried blankets out to the garden, but the raids were so frequent, Cludgy had made the beds in the shelter ready for the next visit.

The Anderson shelter was full of spiders. At first Lindy didn't like them but Cludgy taught her to give them names and she made up stories about them. She remembered how her mother in her letters did the same about the animals near her house in Portsmouth. She climbed up into her bunk above the one where Cludgy slept. There was a separate bed for Arthur, but he was rarely there during a raid as he was out working in his capacity as an Air Raid Warden. At first Lindy found sleeping very difficult as her bunk was very hard, but she got used to it. As soon as her head hit the pillow, she was asleep.

In typical Arthur fashion, the shelter was well built. It was sunken into the ground with the corrugated iron sheets fastened over the top. Around the sides he had stacked small boulders, graded very carefully. He had seen in a book the method used for dry stone walling and used this when he looked after the gardens in the big house. The lady of the house said that they were quaint and looked charming with the climbing roses. On the outside of the shelter, he had added the earth on top of the stones that he had excavated from the floor.

After a few raids and visits to the shelter Lindy put forward an idea. 'Arthur,' she said, 'would it be a good idea if we covered the floor with beach cobbles? Reggie and I could gather some from the beach. There are lots of flat stones there.'

It took quite a few journeys to collect enough stones to cover the whole area. Lindy filled her school bag, whilst Reggie used Auntie Bee's shopping basket. They lugged and heaved their bags up the hill and worked out that more trips carrying less was better than trying to carry too much at once.

'We kept stopping to take a rest, so we decided to do more trips instead,' Lindy explained to Arthur who waited in the shelter for the stones to arrive.

'Cor! You done a real good job there, the floor looks bloomin' marvellous!' said Reggie.

'Yes they do look good, if I say so myself,' said Arthur. 'Let's ask Cludgy what she thinks of all our hard work.'

'Cludgy,' shouted Reggie, 'come and see our bloomin' lovely floor in the shelter!'

Cludgy wiped her hands of the flour she was using and joined the group admiring the floor. 'My, my, that looks lovely. That is the best floor of an Anderson shelter I've ever seen. It's so good that we should ask someone famous to open it.'

'The King', suggested Lindy.

'Churchill! Our Winnie!' said Cludgy.

'Flash Gordon!'

'I'm afraid I don't know his address, Reggie!' said Arthur, 'I think Lord Reggie and Princess Lindy should open it.

'Yes!' said Cludgy, 'a very good idea!'

Arthur found a long strand of ivy. He fixed this to the rivets which held the shelter together. It draped across the door. Cludgy went to the kitchen and collected a pair of scissors. 'Now I suggest,' ventured Cludgy, 'that Reggie cuts the ribbon, oh err ... the ivy, and Lindy gives a speech.'

'What do I say, Cludgy?' asked Lindy.

'Tell them you are pleased to be here and proud to open this Anderson Shelter which has a new floor!'

'Ladies and gentlemen,' she began, 'Err ... Ladies and gentlemen, I just would like to say how happy I am to be here today to open this wonderful, stupendous and marvellous Anderson Shelter, put up by Arthur Sparrow and which has a new floor laid by Arthur and his workers, Reggie and me.'

Cludgy nudged Reggie, 'Go on, cut the ivy,' she said, giving him the scissors.

Reggie held the scissors aloft, waved his arm with a flourish and then cut the stem.

'I declare' said Lindy in a very posh voice, 'this Anderson Shelter, open.'

They all clapped and then laughed. 'Orange Squash all round. I've run out of champagne!' said Cludgy.

'It's going to be lovely to stand on the stone with my bare feet,' said Lindy. They all took their shoes off and tried it out.

'Lovely,' said Cludgy and Arthur together.

'Yes lovely,' said Reggie. 'Can we start work on ours next door now?'

Arthur cleared his throat, 'Err ... we'll think about that tomorrow, shall we?'

'All that work we did just for my feet!' Lindy joked. 'I didn't like the feeling of the bare earth.'

'Necessity is the mother of invention,' Arthur replied.

Lindy took a while to work out what he meant.

12

Transport

There was a knock at the door. Cludgy answered. There was no one there. Just a voice, 'Morning, lovely day, look what I've got!'

Cludgy, followed by Lindy and then Arthur, stepped out, and were faced with a grinning Reggie sitting on a bike. It was a little small for him, but seeing how well he could ride it, he was more than happy.

'Auntie Bee found it in her shed,' he said, 'and the vicar fixed it.'

'Clever man,' said Arthur, 'he preaches reasonable sermons as well. He has many talents, does Mr Peterson our vicar.'

Always impatient Reggie said, 'I want to go for a ride. Will you come Lindy?'

'But I haven't got a bike!'

'No, but you can run, and I'll wait for you.'

Lindy, not wanting to dampen Reggie's enthusiasm and joy, agreed. She had already arranged to run an errand for Cludgy. She was to take some eggs, along with some early potatoes from Arthur's plot to the shop and collect some tins of food. The night before, Reggie had agreed to accompany Lindy, thus lightening the load.

They set off. Lindy carried the eggs very carefully and some of the potatoes. Reggie put the rest of the potatoes in his bag and hung them on the handlebars.

94

'It's a good thing you took the potatoes. The eggs would be scrambled by now if you had them in the bag on your handlebars,' said Lindy

Reggie did as he had said and waited for Lindy to catch up. While he 'waited', he cycled on and returned and did some circles. 'Did you see that Lindy? Clever don't you think?'

'Yes, very good,' Lindy replied.

At the shop they handed over the potatoes and eggs, and received a pack of porridge oats, a tin of custard powder, two tins of milk, baked beans, and some self-raising flour. 'I had a delivery of tinned peaches yesterday. I know that is Mrs Sparrow's favourite so I've added one to your order. I'll take off the amount for the eggs and new potatoes and put the rest on Mrs Sparrow's account,' said the shop keeper. Lindy left the shop with two bulging shopping bags. When they had crossed the road, Reggie gallantly said, 'Gosh, that's rather a lot. Let's take them on my handlebars.'

'Don't you think that is rather a lot to carry on your small bike?' Lindy warned.

'No, no,' Reggie said heroically as he struggled to lift each bag onto the handlebars. He set off. At first it was fine: he was free-wheeling down the road, his legs out to the side like aeroplane wings. However, once he had to pedal his knees hit the bags.

'I'll try with one bag,' he shouted to Lindy.

Lindy took the bag. Reggie started off once more.

95

Again, whilst he freewheeled with his legs out, he was fine. But this time when he started to pedal, his knee hit the bag and he wobbled and fell.

'Good thing I wasn't carrying eggs,' he laughed.

'Did you hurt yourself,' Lindy said a little concerned.

'No, no, just another war wound,' he replied.

'You do have rather a lot of those.'

'I don't think I can manage to pedal with the bag on the handlebars.'

Lindy took the two bags and carried them home, whilst Reggie cycled and circled all the way along the lane. From his vegetable bed, Arthur spotted the two friends return home. Reggie singing and making aeroplane noises, Lindy breathing heavily as she struggled with the two bags. 'I must find a bike for Lindy,' he vowed to himself.

Over the next few days Arthur asked everyone he met if they had an old bike for Lindy. Luckily someone knew someone who knew someone else who had one at the bottom of his garden. Hidden under the curtain of white columbine and blackberry brambles was a medium-sized bicycle. Arthur picked the fruit from the brambles and then he cut away not only the beautiful flowers but the thorny branches to free the bike from its spiky prison of weeds. He didn't show it to Lindy in the state he found it. It looked as though there was no hope for its revival. He didn't want to disappoint her. However, the frame was all right: it was solid, so were the wheels, but the tyres were flat. He took it to the rectory.

'Hello Mr Peterson!' said Arthur. 'I need a little miraculous recovery for this.' He stepped aside to reveal the rather dilapidated machine.'

'Ah! I see. Is it for Lindy?' Mr Peterson asked.

'Yes. Any hope?'

'Bring it around the back and I'll see what we can do.'

Arthur discovered that Reverend George Peterson had first trained as an engineer, before he got his calling to join the church. Together the two men examined the find. Arthur was right; the structure was sound, the frame was good, but the handlebars had lost their shine. All of it needed a good scrub to remove the rust and a coat of paint to brighten it up. The tyres were a problem as they were flat, but the state of the inner tubes was unknown.

'Leave it with me,' said George. 'I'll take pleasure in repairing and renovating this bike for Lindy. Do you know she sings really well? It's a shame that there isn't a choir for girls. She would be an asset.'

Arthur wasn't the only one with a secret. Cludgy had written to Lindy's father about a navy skirt, and he had sent one of Kitty's. It had been worn, but was not worn out. Cludgy unpicked it, washed it and ironed it. Out of the pieces she made a navy skirt for Lindy to wear to school. She left a large hem, so that as Lindy grew, she could let it down. The weather was hot now, and so the jumper was not worn, but just a blouse. Cludgy cut the sleeves off to make it cooler for her. A lot of the girls wore

97

summer dresses in checked gingham. There was no chance of getting any of that.

On Sunday Reverend Peterson preached on the feeding of the five thousand. He spoke about the sharing and giving: not only goods and money, but time. He spoke about the joy that giving can give: joy on the face of the recipient of a gift or a service. This struck home with Lindy, and she remembered Lucy in Portsmouth, what pleasure she had experienced helping her at school, and what pleasure Lucy had felt with Lindy as her friend. She decided to write to her immediately.

Her plans were thwarted. She had just sat down with her pen and paper ready to write her letter, when there was a knock at the door. It was the Reverend George.

'Hello again Lindy, we've got a present for you!' Arthur poked his head around the door. 'Come outside Lindy,' said Arthur.

There in front of the two men was a small bike, cleaned up with shining handlebars and just the right size for Lindy. 'This is for you!' said Reverend George.

Arthur then related how he had acquired the bike, and how George had fixed it.

'Gosh! Oh my goodness. What can I say? You spoke about the joy of giving this morning. Thank you so much. Is it really for me?'

'Glad you enjoyed the sermon!' He was surprised at one so young listening so well. 'Fixing it was purely selfish, as I love tinkering with mechanical things.'

13
The Enemy

Peggy Vaughan, the V.A.D. nurse who had met Lindy from the boat in May, had a sweetheart. She waited for him with her bike at the top of Ronald Road in Little Bridge. She had not let her darling Brian call at the house for her, as her father disapproved of their relationship. In fact, he disapproved of any relationship his daughter may have with any man, in case she left him living alone in his house without the services of a daughter who was a good cook and housekeeper. Her war work was as a Red Cross Nurse. During the air raids she was on standby at the local First Aid Centre.

She had not waited long before Brian turned up.

'Let's go out to the downs, it's a beautiful day,' said Brian.

Peggy turned to look straight at him and mouthed the words 'Wonderful idea, don't go too fast will you.'

Brian understood clearly what she was saying. He had been deafened at the age of seven in Scarborough in December 1914. He was watching three ships in the bay when they fired at the town and hit the house where Brian was living. He was very seriously hurt, and as a result was deaf. 'You are the only person,' he said to Peggy when they first met, 'that I can understand. You speak so clearly.'

Most people when they realised that he had a

99

hearing problem, usually shouted. 'Shouting is useless!' he said. 'I can hear sounds, and together with lip reading I can understand. You, my darling Peggy, do it so well.'

On their bikes the sweethearts cycled off in single file, Brian led, and Peggy followed. Every now and then he turned to smile at Peggy who was just behind. They stopped at the top of Rolling Road. Peggy caught up. 'Anything wrong?' she asked.

'How do you fancy going as far as Brading Down?'

'OK. Is it far?' said Peggy knowing full well that she would go anywhere with Brian.

'No, no,' Brian assured her, 'you can manage.'

She smiled at him and together the sweethearts cycled off in the beautiful sunshine, happy to be together.

Also planning a bike trip was Reggie. The bikes had created a new playground for the friends. They had cycled all around the village. They even took them down the steep hill in Ladies Lane to the beach. The hill posed a problem, as it was too steep to ride down. Reggie tried it and only just managed to stop.

'Good job I've good brakes,' he said.

Equally the incline was too great to pedal up, so they both had to push their bikes.

'There's no use in riding our bikes to the beach,' concluded Lindy. 'The hill is too steep. It's dangerous to ride the bikes going down and far too steep for us to pedal up.'

Each time, as they left on yet another adventure,

Cludgy added a message of safety: 'Take care! **And don't go too far**.' The expression 'too far', according to Reggie hadn't actually got a distance.

Lindy was taller than Reggie, and her bike was bigger with larger wheels. She could easily go faster than Reggie, whose legs were pedaling at twice the speed of Lindy's. This didn't stop him from going 'far too far'.

They crossed the main road at the top of the hill and cycled towards the open country and the downs. Every time they got to a junction Lindy would call out, 'Surely we've gone far enough! Reggie - let's turn around.'

Reggie appeared not to hear. He didn't turn, he just cycled on and on. Lindy followed.

They reached the end of Rolling Road where Peggy and Brian stood with their bikes together. Brian held Peggy's hand and she rested her head on Brian's shoulder. In silence they looked at the view. 'It's so beautiful,' she said. 'It's so peaceful. You'd hardly know there was a war on.'

That peace was shattered suddenly as an aeroplane flew overhead, closely followed by another plane. The sweethearts dropped their bikes to the ground and turned to look for a place they could shelter.

Just then they saw and heard Reggie who was dancing in the road. His arms were outstretched as he sang: 'That's one of our boys! Go get the Jerry! Hooray! Hooray for the RAF!'

'That's Reggie!' said Peggy, 'And Lindy is over there.'

101

'You grab the girl!' shouted Brian, 'I'll get the boy! Go back to the hollow over there. He turned around to Reggie. 'Come here you little idiot! You'll get yourself killed!'

'It's Miss Vaughan,' yelled Lindy.

'Lindy, come with me' said Peggy as they ran towards the hollow. They found an overhanging rock and lay flat underneath it. Brian followed, carrying Reggie over his shoulder as would a fireman, and laid him down next to the others. Making his body as big as he could he lay flat, covering the group. 'Cover your faces and lie still.'

Like a morbid game of Hide and Seek, they lay still. Reggie couldn't resist, he turned his head, opened one eye and saw the planes performing an evil dance in the sky.

'Will my bike be OK?' whispered Lindy.

'She's worried about her bike,' Peggy relayed to Brian.

'Forget your bike! Goodness me, you could have been killed,' said Brian rather crossly.

'But I've only just been given it,' she whimpered.

They seemed to be lying there for ages, but it could only have been a few minutes.

'I think they've gone,' Brian announced. 'There they are! Going over Ashey Down.' Sure enough the party watched as the RAF plane chased the German firing all the way until they were out of sight. One of the planes must have crashed as they saw black smoke rising from the

103

other side of the hill.

Reggie got up and did his dance again. 'I hope that was the German. That's our boys, the RAF. They got him! That's one less plane to attack us again.'

'One less pilot too,' said Peggy. 'There was a man in that plane, whose mother, sister or sweetheart will never see him again.'

'I think it was the German plane that went down, as he was in front and our chap was chasing him,' said Brian.

'My bike, I must get my bike, Miss Vaughan.' Lindy said anxiously. She turned and ran back out of the hollow and found her bike where she had laid it down.

'It's a lovely bike!' said Peggy.

'Arthur found it and the vicar fixed it for me. Aren't they kind?' Lindy was shaking and Reggie was quite subdued.

'You two are a long way from home,' said Brian. 'I think it's time we all went back.'

'I didn't want to go this far!' said Lindy. Tears started to come to her eyes. 'I kept telling him to stop and go back. He just kept going on and on.' Now tears started to fall. Peggy put her arms around her. 'I mustn't cry, I must be brave,' Lindy kept repeating.

'Cry all you like Lindy,' Peggy said as she cuddled her in her arms.

Reggie thought it best to keep quiet now. He had been silly to go this far, and had been ticked off, and now felt very foolish.

'Come on Reggie, act like a man!' said Brian. 'We must get these lovely ladies home.'

Peggy led the procession, followed by Reggie, Lindy and then Brian. He wanted to keep an eye on everyone. They arrived home just as an air raid warning was being sounded. Reggie ran next door.

'I must get to the first aid centre,' said Peggy.

'Not now,' said Arthur 'Let's all get into the air raid shelter.'

'Yes' said Cludgy, 'there's plenty of time when this is finished. You must stay here.'

The bikes were abandoned, and they all squeezed into the Anderson Shelter.

'Nice floor!' said Brian.

Like most of the raids there was little to hear and see. There were explosions far away, but not too close. They heard a few planes overhead, but nothing was dropped nearby.

'They're not interested in Little Bridge today!' said Arthur.

'Thank goodness!' said Cludgy.

They settled down. 'Did you enjoy your ride, Lindy?' asked Cludgy in a quiet moment.

Lindy burst into tears.

14
Holes on the beach.

The other beach became a popular venue for the two friends. They cycled the short distance and then wheeled their bikes down the cobbly lane.

Reggie always tried to freewheel down the foot path. At the start of it, he adeptly manoeuvred his bike over and around the stones, but, as the stones got bigger, he came to a standstill. Never to be beaten he moved the bike beyond each stone and got on again. On this day where the path got smoother and steeper, Reggie's confidence increased, and he went faster until he came to another abrupt stop and he fell off sideways.

'Good thing I wasn't going at maximum speed, I would have gone over the handlebars,' he proudly announced.

'Good job too!' said Lindy who was walking her bike and easily kept up with Reggie. 'Perhaps it's better to walk your bike from now on, it gets quite steep just around the bend.'

'OK! I'll walk now,' Reggie conceded.

They leant their bikes against the bank opposite the smelly bog and walked the last few steps to the large oak tree where the path splits. Lindy and Reggie went either side and jumped down at the same time. They laughed at their co-ordinated action.

The tide was out, revealing a large expanse of

seaweed, rocks and blue slipper clay. 'It doesn't look so pretty when the tide isn't in,' said Lindy.

'Pretty?' said Reggie.

'Yes! Pretty! Well, not so inviting then.'

They took off their sandals and walked along the high tide water mark.

'Look!' said Lindy. 'What's going on here? There's a hole in the soft sand. And here's another one,' she continued.

'And another!'

'They're all over the place. Whatever's been happening?' queried Lindy.

They stood still and turned around and saw that there were holes that stretched all along the beach. They walked from one hole to another peering in each of them. Reggie found a stick and poked the bottom of each.

'Who dug these? What on earth are they for? They're all over the place.' said Lindy. 'They all look roughly the same size too.'

'Do you think they may be making a mine field?' said Reggie.

'But why are they empty?'

Reggie, now speaking with an air of authority, said, 'Obviously they'll be coming back later to put the mines in.'

'Good thing there are no mines in them now, after you've poked around in each,' Lindy said. 'If they mined this beach, we won't be able to come here and play.'

107

Sadly, the two friends walked along the beach. They climbed over the flat stones, and walked in and out of the stakes that had been put there a long time ago to allow the fishing nets to dry. Lindy looked over the water to Portsmouth and thought of her father. He would love to come to this beach, she thought. At the very end, they turned a corner and they could see the other beach. They discovered that they could walk there, but only when the tide was far out. More importantly, they had to negotiate the blue slipper clay.

'Not a nice walk!' said Lindy.

'No, not a nice walk indeed,' agreed Reggie. 'Look at the clay, we'd probably sink up to at least our knees, maybe our waists or shoulders and maybe never be seen again.' His voice reached a crescendo as he spoke.

'Oh do shut up Reggie.'

They turned around and started the long walk back along the sand. In the far distance, they spotted two soldiers jumping down onto the beach by the oak tree.

'Look soldiers! Perhaps they're coming back to lay the mines, Lindy.'

'We'd better get off the beach then,' she said.

Behind the two soldiers were two girls. Very gallantly, the soldiers helped them negotiate the small step down on to the sand.

'I hardly think they're going to lay mines with their girl-friends, do you?' said Lindy.

'Maybe we've got it all wrong? I hope so.'

The two couples split and, holding hands walked along the beach. They each found places to stop. The soldiers gallantly took off their jackets, laid them on the sand and then the four of them sat down and in couples cuddled up.

At the oak tree, Lindy and Reggie climbed up the bank and started walking back to where they had left their bikes. They heard some men's voices and saw them coming towards them. With them were four very excitable small dogs that bounded towards the children. All four were barking loudly.

'Don't worry,' said one of the men, 'their bark is worse than their bite. I mean, they don't bite at all!'

Lindy and Reggie, both a little shocked by the over-exuberant animals, stood back each side of the path to let them through. For some unknown reason, all four dogs bounded towards Reggie. With tails wagging the four dogs jumped on him. He staggered as he stepped backwards towards the fence. He tried to get further away from the pack by taking another step, but this led him to hit the fence post. Unfortunately, this particular post was rotten, and snapped at the base. Behind this fence was the black smelly bog, and Reggie fell backwards, taking the four dogs with him into the quagmire. They all ended up in the smelly sludge.

'Dasher, Churchill, come here!' shouted one of the men. 'I'm so sorry. They won't hurt you; they just want to play.'

Dasher, Churchill, Prince and Sausage obediently recovered themselves, leaving Reggie lying in the bog. When the dogs reached the path, they stood and shook themselves all over everyone. Reggie lay still, his whole body submerged, except, fortunately, for his face, which appeared pure white against the black mud that covered the rest of him.

The two men each took one of Reggie's hands and hauled him out.

'Thank you mister,' Reggie said.

He stood up, covered with black smelly mud.

'Eugh! You don't half stink, Reggie!' said Lindy.

'I'm not surprised,' said one of the men.

'Are you alright?' said the other. 'Do you live far away?'

'I'm soaked to the skin!' wailed Reggie.

'It's alright, we live nearby. Just by the church,' said Lindy. 'I'll be with him. We were on our way home anyway.'

Reggie wiped his hands on some leaves and grass that grew at the side of the path. 'I don't want to get my handlebars dirty,' he said.

'You don't half smell awful' repeated Lindy, trying to stifle a laugh.

'I know, I know! Don't go on!'

Lindy couldn't help giggling as her friend did look funny. He was covered in black mud from head to toe.

'It's a good thing your face didn't go under the water.

110

There's no mud on your eyes, nose, mouth or chin.' Lindy tried to reassure her friend.

Reggie was without his usual cheeky demeanour. 'Stop laughing,' he said angrily. 'It's not funny! I've been attacked by a pack of dangerous hounds.'

'No, you haven't! You've been jumped on by four friendly small dogs,' Lindy said, 'who just wanted to play.'

At the top of the footpath, Lindy mounted her bike to cycle the last few yards home. She expected Reggie to get on his bike too.

'I don't want to muck up my saddle. I'll only have to clean the handlebars now,' he said.

Just as they passed the church, the air raid siren sounded.

'Not another one!' said Lindy.

Cludgy came out into the lane and called them in.

'Betsy is at the shops. Reggie, you'll have to come into our shelter with us,' she instructed. Then she caught sight of the mud-covered boy.

'Reggie, what on earth … Where on earth have you been? You're all covered in black mud.'

'I know, I know!' groaned Reggie.

'Get into the shelter quickly.'

They hadn't been in the shelter long before it became apparent where he had been, as the smell intensified in the small, enclosed environment.

'He needs a bath,' said Cludgy and Lindy in unison.

'I know, I know. Don't go on so!'

111

Later in the evening, during supper, Lindy related the tale of the visit to the beach and the holes and how Reggie had fallen in the stagnant smelly bog.

'I don't know the names of the two men, but I've remembered the names of the four dogs. They were Dasher, Churchill, Prince and Sausage.'

'Ah ha!' said Arthur. 'Do you want to know what those holes were all about, Lindy? It's those dogs. They get down on the beach and they dig the holes.'

'But there were lots of holes all along the beach. How could they dig so many?' questioned Lindy.

'Well, there are four dogs and if they dig five holes each, that's 20,' replied Arthur. 'And if they dig one more each ...'

'That's 24 holes!' said Lindy, 'I know my times tables!'

That night Lindy wrote one of her best ever letters to her father.

15
Air Raids

Activity in the skies over the Island intensified. Throughout the summer the lives of the islanders were continually disrupted by the sound of the air raid warnings. Arthur was constantly out during the raids to help where needed. Cludgy worried, but hid her concerns by busying herself with looking after Lindy.

The disruption was constant. If you weren't disrupted by the warning, you were concerned whether to start a job, ever fearful that you could not finish it because there may be a warning. Baking was a problem for Cludgy. She saved up the family's precious coupons to have enough for a cake – a luxury that Arthur and Lindy loved.

'Shall I bake this cake now or leave it? I don't want to have to take it out of the oven if there's a warning.'

Lindy and Arthur couldn't offer any advice.

Roasting a joint of meat wasn't a problem. There were never enough coupons between the three of them to buy a piece of meat large enough to be called a joint of meat.

Lindy was used to the routine. At school, they quickly lined up and walked in crocodile formation to the air raid shelter in the playground.

Texi was very used to the raids, and as soon as the siren was sounded, he went immediately to his basket in

113

the shelter. Invariably he was there before anyone else, even before Cludgy had picked up her basket of provisions and Lindy had got downstairs.

'If they bombed the school, we wouldn't be able to go to school,' said Reggie one day when in the shelter. Whilst there the children often recited poems, sang songs and, worst of all, recited their times tables.

'Bomb the school?' Lindy stared at him with a look of disdain.

'Don't look at me like that! Well! We wouldn't. Would we? Then we could play all day.'

'You'd get bored,' Lindy whispered.

Activity over the island occurred throughout the day or night. The children played near the house. The furthest they went was to the beach at the bottom of the hill. They didn't go to the other beach, which they now named "Smelly Bog Beach".

'We should name this beach too' said Reggie one day.

'That's easy, it's the beach near the little bridge, so it should be called "Little Bridge Beach".

One day, just before the wail of the siren was sounded, they stood on Little Bridge Beach looking across the sea to Portsmouth. In the far distance Lindy could see smoke rising from the port.

'My dad's over there, fighting fires and helping people,' said Lindy.

Just then the air raid warning sounded.

114

'Come on, we've got to get back!' shouted Reggie.

'I wish he was here with me!' said Lindy.

The wail of the siren was worse at night. Lindy hated being disturbed when she was in a deep sleep. So used to the routine she walked downstairs one night holding her pillow against her face.

'Are you alright?' asked Cludgy.

'Yes fine, I've just got the pillow to the right shape to be really comfortable.' She continued to hold the pillow in the same place down the stairs, out of the kitchen door across the path and into the shelter. Then she carefully placed the pillow on the top bunk, climbed up and positioned her head in the exact place she had had it in her bed. Cludgy put the blanket over her, and Lindy promptly went to sleep.

Lindy and her father continued to write letters to each other. Lindy's were full of news about her and Reggie. Her father's were full of drawings. When she told him about the bike and the episode with the muddy bog, a pin man riding a bike appeared in his next letter. The pin man was being sprayed by a fireman. There was a speech bubble coming from his mouth. 'Phew it stinks. I must get all the black mud off the bike,' it said.

Drawings indicating Lindy always had a triangle for a skirt, ones for Reggie had two short oblongs on his legs to indicate shorts.

Whenever there had been a fierce raid on the city, a letter arrived a couple of days later. It didn't say that he

115

was all right, but she knew and was reassured.

Dangers were ever present. Peggy Vaughan was walking up the main road, when a Messerschmitt followed her and began firing. Luckily a soldier was nearby: his training and sharp reaction kicked in; he grabbed her and threw her into a ditch under a hedge. They were both unharmed. But the story shot around the village, and Arthur wisely concluded that the Germans would follow main roads to get to their destination, so it was best to stick to the side roads and country lanes.

A German plane crash-landed in the south of the island. This was put on display at the fire station in Newport. The plane was relatively undamaged so, as a fundraiser for the Spitfire fund, people were charged sixpence to sit in the cockpit. The children wanted to go and have a look.

'You'll be too far away from home,' Arthur wisely said, 'and you don't know when there may be another raid.'

The children had to make do with a report in the local paper.

The route for planes to Portsmouth and Southampton was directly over the island. The Spitfires and Hurricane planes weaved in and out of the German aircraft formations, firing as they went. These dog fights took place a great deal over the area. British planes and enemy fighters crash-landed in fields, and some went down in the sea. Bombs fell in Ryde and Newport and caused much damage. There was a massive raid on Southampton one day. The Germans were hoping that this would put the ship building and industry out of action. Many died that day. At school, prayers were said for those poor people who died. Not knowing any of those people had less of an effect on the children than the prayers said for Isabella Black. She had come down from London to escape the bombing. Isabella was a school mate and had died when a bomb fell directly on the house in which she stayed. The sight of the empty desk troubled the class.

It was an upsetting time for Lindy. She wanted to concentrate on her schoolwork. Miss Simons was enjoying setting and marking more advanced work for her pupil. If the siren was sounded, Lindy had to leave her books quickly, but if it was quiet, she was forever listening for the wail to begin.

At every opportunity, Lindy went down to the beach by the little bridge to gaze across the water and look at Portsmouth. She strained her eyes. She would worry if there was smoke seen rising as she knew that was where her father was fighting the fires. She dreamed that she could fly over the sea and watch her father at work.

Cludgy was aware of Lindy's worries. It was no use telling her that all would be well. She didn't know: she couldn't know; because no one knew if they were safe or not. Apart from the worry of being blown up by a bomb, there was a threat of invasion.

'I want to be with my Daddy if the Germans come Cludgy,' she said one day out of the blue.

'I'll do my best to make that happen,' she replied.

Cludgy knew when to say nothing, or when just to cuddle Lindy when she was near to tears. Lindy's father always wrote straight away after he had finished work on a particular difficult fire or bombed building. He always found something funny to draw in pin men. He found it hard to draw a picture of a lady who refused to leave her burning house without her teeth. He had had to go into the house and collect them for her from the bedside table.

He didn't tell her of the harrowing times, of how he had to retrieve bodies from the wreckage of their homes. He never let on just how tired he was at the end of a shift, how the team often sat still in silence, saying nothing of the awful work they had done.

Sometimes his letters were very short. Lindy knew he was busy; she didn't mind, just holding his letter in her hands was enough to know he was safe.

Reggie, unbeknown to him, was a great help to Lindy. Playing together was a distraction. They had become quite close. They both came from Portsmouth, albeit from very different areas. They were becoming like brother and sister. Reggie had such an imaginative mind that Lindy never knew what they would be doing next.

16
A Good Turn

After one daylight raid, Reggie knocked on the kitchen door just after the all-clear was sounded. It was late afternoon. He was without his bike.

'Where's your bike?' asked Lindy.

'The back tyre is flat,' he said. 'Probably got a puncture.'

'Or maybe,' suggested Lindy, 'it just needs to be pumped up.'

'Maybe if I leave it, someone else will pump it up!'

'You lazy thing!' scolded Lindy. 'Alright, we'll go for a walk.'

As they left, Cludgy gave her usual warning 'Don't go too far.'

'We're not likely to. We've no bikes,' Lindy said.

They ambled past the church and on towards Smelly Bog beach. 'Shall we go down there?' suggested Lindy.

'No. Let's aim for the White Gate at the end of Quarry Lane. That's not too far, is it?'

'No, I suppose not.'

They took the lane through the woods where they had played Kick the Can. Coming out of the path into the road, they saw a goat by the red post box. He was munching on the grass around its base. They looked around. There was no-one else there.

'Hello little goat!' said Lindy, approaching the animal

119

gingerly. 'You must be lost.'

'Of course he's lost, silly,' said Reggie. 'There's no-one else here and he's all alone.'

The goat was wearing a halter, with a broken piece of rope attached to it.

'Where do you come from, little goat?' said Lindy.

'He's not going to answer you, is he? He's a goat.'

Lindy looked under the goat carefully, 'I think you'll find this goat is a she.'

'Okay I think **she** belongs to the big house behind where we live.'

'That's right,' said Lindy. 'They keep her for the milk she can provide.'

With all this attention, the goat decided to make a bolt for it, and ran off down the road towards the White Gate.

'We must take her home,' said Lindy.

'Someone might steal her,' suggested Reggie.

They ran after the animal that fortunately had found some more grass to eat and had stopped.

'Who's going to hold the straps that are round her head?' asked Reggie.

'That's called a halter. I'll try,' said Lindy, feeling she was the older of the two of them, and therefore should be more responsible.

'Here Goaty-Goaty, come to Lindy. I'm going to take you home.' Carefully and slowly, Lindy approached the animal and took hold of the broken rope and tried to

120

move her back to the road. Goaty-Goaty had a different idea and stood firm. She was going nowhere.

'Oh come on, Goaty-Goaty. There's a good Goaty-Goaty. Come with Lindy, I'm going to take you home. Oh please, Goaty-Goaty!'

'She's not budging!' said Reggie.

Every time Lindy caught hold of the rope, the goat tossed her head, pulling the rope from Lindy's hand, and she moved away to another juicy bit of grass.

'I've an idea!' said Reggie, 'She likes the grass so we'll tempt her with a bunch of that. I'll walk in front and you shoo her along from behind.'

This worked for a while, but Goaty-Goaty decided she could get her own grass quite adequately by herself.

'It'd help if I had a rope so I could lead her.' said Lindy. 'The rope she has at the moment is far too short. My hands keep slipping off.'

The two children stood and thought for a moment.

'We need a long piece of rope,' repeated Lindy. They looked around.

'I know what!' announced Reggie. 'My braces will do. They're long enough. We could tie them to the halter.'

'Won't your shorts fall down?' asked Lindy.

'Nah! They'll rest on me hips.'

Reggie took off his braces. His shorts dropped quite a few inches down his legs, finishing well below his knees. They only just balanced on his hips. Lindy tied the braces to the halter.

121

'There!' she announced. 'Get some more grass and I'll lead her as you walk in front, tempting her with the juicy grass.'

In procession Lindy, Goaty-Goaty and Reggie in front, now holding up his shorts with one hand and a bunch of grass with the other, walked along the road.

'Come on Goaty-Goaty, off you go. There's a good Goaty-Goaty,' they chanted.

Goaty-Goaty stopped. Obviously, she had had her fill of juicy grass. She was going no further. As Lindy pulled, Reggie got behind her and pushed, but Goaty-Goaty stood still. The two children stopped and thought.

'I've another idea!' announced Reggie.

Lindy sighed!

'I've heard that goats have taken clothes from people's washing lines and eaten them. We could tempt her with that,' he suggested.

'What bit of clothing are you suggesting? I'm not going to take off my dress!' said Lindy firmly.

'No, I'll take off one of my socks, that'll do!' he said.

Reggie sat down and took off one of his shoes and then a sock. He put the shoe back on again. 'I wish I'd worn my sandals instead of my lace-ups,' he muttered.

The procession resumed. Lindy held on firmly to Reggie's braces that were attached to the goat by the halter. Reggie was in front, holding his shorts up with one hand and holding his bright red sock in the air with the other. It worked! Back they went up the road from the

White Gate, up past the red post box, along the path which passed the site of the Kick the Can game and finally into the road leading to the church and their homes. Goaty-Goaty happily walked along between the two children who were chanting the encouraging phrases all the way.

'Come on Goaty-Goaty! Nearly home Goaty-Goaty! You're a good Goaty-Goaty! Keep going Goaty-Goaty!'

Cludgy heard them coming down the lane and went out to see. 'What on earth have you got there?' she said.

'It's Goaty-Goaty, I mean it's a goat,' Lindy replied.

'It belongs to the big house behind ours. They keep it for milk!' Reggie said. 'We found her in Quarry Road by the post box.'

Cludgy took a closer look! 'No, it isn't! I mean it is a goat, but it doesn't belong to the big house. It belongs to the monks at the Abbey on the other side of the White Gate. This isn't Isobel from the big house, she's white. This one has brown markings. I've just seen Isobel in the garden of the big house.'

'We did find her in Quarry Road, this side of the White Gate,' said Lindy. 'Someone must have left the gate open for her to slip through.'

Silence followed, as all three suddenly realised they had to get Goaty-Goaty back to where she lived. They had to go past where they had found her and further on down to the Abbey. They stood looking at each other.

'Arthur will know what to do' said Cludgy.

123

17

Pieter

It was just an ordinary day, if anyone could say 'ordinary' when there were constant air raids taking place, dog fights overhead and the possibility of bombs being dropped somewhere on the Island.

Reggie called for Lindy as he usually did. He knocked on the door and asked, 'Can Lindy come out to play?' as he normally did. It was a lovely day, bright sunshine with a few wispy clouds floating above.

'What a lovely day,' Cludgy said, as she always said if the weather was fine.

'You'd hardly think there was a war on,' commented Arthur as he always said on a fine quiet day.

Lindy decided to wear her old school summer dress that Cludgy had adapted. She had taken the sleeves out and made it into a sundress. Reggie had dressed himself in a shirt and a pair of shorts that were far too big for him. They were hand-me-downs given to Betsy for him.

'They are a little big,' she said, 'but he will grow into them.' He hadn't yet grown enough for them to look smart, but they were corduroy and in a lovely shade of dark red. He liked them and wore them often. They were baggy but were held up with his faithful braces.

'Fortunately,' he said, 'no damage was caused by using them as a rope to lead the goat.'

They turned left out of the path and walked down to

124

their favourite beach. Lindy loved it. She sat still and gazed over the Solent to Portsmouth where her father was. It was a favourite of Reggie's too, as there were rocks to climb and a stream to jump over.

This little stream spread out when it reached the beach, especially when the tide was out, and so he had to make a bigger stride to get over it. Lindy had jumped it the first time she came there. She failed on her second jump and got wet feet. She hadn't attempted it again and was more careful now. Reggie loved to practise his long jump over it. If he managed it, he shouted, 'Look at me, I'm a champion!' He would then run around arms in the air, cheering himself. If he didn't manage to jump the great distance and landed in the water, he got wet feet!

Lindy sat on the sand as she always did and looked over to Portsmouth. It was such an ordinary day she pondered about what she could tell her father in her next letter to him?

Dear Daddy, she said to herself, *it's a very ordinary day, the sun is shining. Reggie and I went to the beach.* She laughed at herself.

Reggie joined her. 'Are both feet wet, or just the one?' she asked.

'Both!' he casually said. 'But they'll dry, it's such a lovely day!'

'Take off your shoes and they may dry quicker,' Lindy suggested. She had already taken her shoes off.

With sand between their toes, they sat quietly. They

saw so much of each other that they really had nothing to say that was new. There had been an air raid the night before, but both children had slept through it. The all-clear had sounded just after dawn, so not wanting to disturb Lindy, Cludgy had left her blissfully sleeping in the shelter.

'I wonder if Daddy was working last night?' said Lindy. 'I wonder if the air raid was because the planes were going to Portsmouth.'

'Or Southampton!' suggested Reggie. 'My mum's in Southampton.'

'I thought you came from Portsmouth?' said Lindy

'I do. But she works in a factory, and she was ordered to go to Southampton. She's living with her sister, my Auntie Joan.'

'I have an Auntie Joan; well I have an **Aunt** Joan. She's my father's sister. She came to live with us for a while after Mummy died.'

Reggie fell silent. He didn't know what to say. He had never met anyone whose mother had died.

It was Reggie who finally broke the silence. 'She's building Spitfires!'

'What, all by herself?' said Lindy.

'No silly, with other ladies.'

'She must work in a large factory then. Spitfires look small in the sky, but they're really quite big,' remarked Lindy.

'That's funny! She said that she's working in a

126

laundry. I know it well, it's near where my Auntie Joan lives.'

'Well! She won't have far to walk to work then. Did you think she was washing sheets and clothes?'

'I don't know!' replied Reggie. 'Washing dirty clothes is very different from making planes.'

The two friends fell silent again as they sat gazed out to sea. The water was still, the sun beat down and there was a slight breeze enough to cool their faces. It was idyllic!

'You would hardly know,' said Reggie repeating Arthur's statement, 'that there was a war on.'

'It's a **shame** that there **is** a war on. It's so warm, I want to go for a paddle!' remarked Lindy.

The tide was in, so they only had to make a short walk over the sand to the water's edge.

'Remember Arthur's warning,' said Lindy, 'we must only go in up to our ankles.'

Reggie, however had already been in the stream water up to his knees. The water was warm and so inviting.

'I long to get in and swim,' said Lindy.

'Can you swim?' asked Reggie.

'Yes, they taught us at school. Can you swim?'

'Yes, I can. I wasn't taught though. I fell in at Southsea and soon learnt! I was under the water when I thought at the time, I'd better do something or I'd drown. So, I moved my arms and legs – came up to surface and paddled to the shore.'

Lindy looked at him astounded. 'Really?'

'Yes, really!' he replied.

In silence, they walked up and down the shoreline, the wet sand squidging between their toes. It was quiet and the sea was warm.

It was Reggie who noticed it first.

'Look out there. There's something in the water.'

'I see it. What on earth is it? Could it be an animal, a dog or a horse for instance?' suggested Lindy. 'It's not moving! Maybe it's a bag, or clothing.'

'A horse! Lindy, what would a horse be doing near the sea and getting himself deep enough to drown? It could of course be a dead body!' suggested Reggie.

'Oh, my goodness, I do hope not,' Lindy said.

The children watched as whatever it was it was floating motionless. All of a sudden to their surprise, whatever it was rolled over, stopped, looked around and began to swim towards them. Lindy and Reggie jumped. It must have dawned on them at the same time. 'It's a man!' they said in unison.

'He can't have come for a bathe?' said Lindy.

'Don't be daft, he's got all his clothes on!'

Transfixed at what they saw, the children stood motionless as the object came closer to them.

'One thing's for sure, he's not dead. I don't like this,' said Lindy, 'I want to go home!'

'Don't worry, I'm here to protect you!' said Reggie

boldly. 'By the time he gets to shore, if he makes it to shore, we could run away, and he'll be so tired he won't be able to catch us.'

'Could it be a service man, a soldier, sailor or an airman?' Lindy suggested.

'If it's an airman, maybe he had to bail out as his Spitfire fell into the sea!' said Reggie. 'He must have chased the German firing all the time and then caught a bullet which destroyed his engine! and … and …'

'Reggie, shut up! You're making it all up. I want to go home.'

'Let's wait and see what he does.'

As he got closer, the children moved back to where they had left their things. They put on their shoes, preparing themselves to run if needs be. Suddenly he shouted.

'Hello there!' The children looked at each other, they were a little less afraid as he spoke English.

'Could he be a German?' suggested Lindy.

'I don't know,' said Reggie.

The children were confused, as they could see nothing of a uniform to identify him as he was floating.

'I want to go home,' repeated Lindy.

'He's speaking in English!' said Reggie.

'Hello there! Good morning, lovely day!' said the airman. He spoke with a strange accent. Nothing like people they knew.

'Are we being invaded?' said Lindy.

'I don't think so. They would need more soldiers than just one!' Reggie spoke with authority.

'Maybe he's in the advance party!'

'Don't be silly!' Reggie laughed.

The man swam to shallow water and then pulled himself further onto the beach and sat in the surf.

'He's a pilot!' said Reggie.

Even though he was sitting, it was obvious he was tall. He smiled and ran his hands through his fair hair. He took off his life vest and then the truth was revealed.

'He's not one of ours!' Reggie continued. 'Look at the colour of his uniform. That's not RAF blue. I know that for sure!'

'I want to go home,' repeated Lindy

'The sea is so beautiful, don't you think?' the man continued, 'It's lucky I had to ditch on such a fine day.'

'He must be a German then!' said Lindy.

The children did not know what to think or do. Lindy clutched onto Reggie arm tightly.

'If we run away, he might shoot us,' she said.

'Nah - if he has a gun, it won't fire as it's been in the water for too long.'

'How do you know that?' said Lindy.

'He can't chase us as I think he has a wounded leg,' noticed Reggie. 'He was dragging himself along and not standing up.'

The children remained close together and motionless.

'Ah! I know,' said the German, remembering his training. 'I must surrender to you, and tell you only my name, my rank and my serial number.'

He wasn't aggressive or horrid. He was smiling, and was quite calm and normal. His knowledge of the English language was good. but his accent was not like anything the children had heard before.

He turned to Lindy and Reggie and sat straight up. He saluted them and said, 'I surrender, my name is Pieter Krupper. Here is my …' as he put his hand on his holster, undid the soggy leather and took out the gun. The children gasped and took a step back.

'Oh Reggie, I want to go home.'

He stopped and looked at Lindy and Reggie who were now shaking with fear.

'I do not want to give a weapon to a child.' He held the gun by the barrel. 'It will not work,' he reassured his stationary audience. 'It has been in the sea too long'.

'Told you!' bragged Reggie.

'I won't give you the gun because it could be dangerous. I'll bury it in the sand and cover it with this big stone,' the airman said. He dragged himself further up the beach towards Lindy and Reggie, who in turn moved further back away from him. They held hands and cowered together. The airman dug a small hole, long enough to take the gun and its barrel. He put it in the hole, covered it with sand. It made a slight heap, so he patted it down, as if he were making a sandcastle. A large

131

flat stone was nearby, so he put that on the top and pushed it down. Then he added more stones.

'There, it is safe now,' he said, 'I like building sandcastles, do you?'

The friends relaxed a little.

'Can you walk?' asked Reggie.

'Yes normally, but I don't think so at the moment. A Spitfire shot at my Messerschmitt. The engine got most of the bullets, but I got one in my leg.'

Lindy and Reggie felt a little more calm. He had buried his gun and couldn't walk. The situation was a little safer.

'I managed to land on the calm sea, climb out and float, and here I am.'

'Oh! That's good,' said Lindy.

'So, you didn't drown then?' added Reggie.

'No, but my plane did,' said the airman continuing with Reggie's joke. 'It sank!'

'Let me introduce myself to you. My name is Pieter. Will you tell me your names? I am a member of the German Luftwaffe, but I am half Dutch. My father is German, my mother is Dutch. I am married to Susannah who is Swiss and have two children called Robert and Mary.'

'Those are very English names,' remarked Lindy.

'Before the war I was in England studying at Cambridge University. I met my wife there. Our children have English names because we like England and wanted

132

to come and live here. Then the war came, and I was called up and taught how to fly.'

'You're telling us far more than just your name and number,' said Lindy.

'Oh yes, but I don't like war. You probably don't like it either. So, we have that in common. I will be taken as a prisoner of war and be looked after until they stop fighting!'

'Aren't you worried about your wife and children left in Germany?'

'No, they are in Switzerland with my parents-in-law. We saw what was coming and I got them to safety, before all the fighting started.'

Lindy and Reggie introduced themselves and explained their situation and that they were evacuees.

His attitude of not caring for all the fighting and bombing that was going on in the papers, on the radio and over their heads on the island, worried Reggie. Soldiers, airmen and sailors should be tough, gruff people wanting to protect their country by killing others. Pieter was not like that at all. He was a friendly chap, like an uncle, who comes at Christmas and brings presents.

Pieter continued and told them how he came to be on this beach. 'I had to protect the bombers that were bombing Southampton. A Spitfire chased me and fired at me. When my engine was hit I lost power, but I managed to glide down and land my plane quite nicely on the surface of the sea. I opened my cockpit and despite my injured leg I managed to climb out and get into the water. It was not very cold, so I floated on my back and the current brought me here. Then I saw you. So, I thought it a good place to go ashore. I am so glad I found you two, you are so helpful. But now we have a problem, ja? How are we going to get me to the authorities? I am in no fit state to walk a distance, and I have lost my boots.'

The three of them sat and pondered as to what to do and how to help Pieter.

18
The Capture

The decision as to what to do next depended mostly on trusting Pieter. Lindy and Reggie saw him as a gentle, kind and considerate man. They sat on the beach together as they would if they were there to have a picnic.

'We've got to hand you over to the authorities!' Lindy said. 'And there's no way we can call for help or find anyone who can go for help here on the beach. There are only the three of us, and you can't walk.'

'If Lindy and I leave to get help,' reasoned Reggie, 'then we've to trust you to stay here until we get back!'

'Oh, that's easy,' said Pieter. 'I would enjoy just resting on this pretty beach!'

'But if you're spotted before we've spoken to the police, they may shoot, before they understand that you're not armed, and have surrendered to us,' said Lindy. 'I suggest that Reggie runs on ahead and gets help, while I stay with you Pieter. Perhaps we could make a start along the long path from the beach.'

Reggie rushed off and Pieter, his arm over Lindy's shoulder, made a slow start at walking without shoes along the flagstone track to the main path. He managed to put his bad left leg on the ground, as with Lindy's help he could hop with his right. They had managed halfway when Reggie came bounding back. 'I saw Mr Peterson,' he said in-between breaths, 'and I told him all about

136

Pleter. He's going to ring for the police.'

Lindy prepared to help Pieter walk along the rest of the path.

'How can I help you, Pieter?' asked Reggie.

'If I put my hand on your shoulder, I can use you like a walking stick.' The three set off. Pieter took a step with his bad leg, and with support from his stick, namely Reggie, he managed to walk his right leg forward.

'This is so much better,' said Pieter. 'Thank you, Reggie.'

All three were exhausted when they reached the end. 'I think we need a rest here,' said Lindy.

'Thank you so much,' said Pieter. 'I could not have managed that without you two. You are very kind. I shall always remember you.'

They leant on the bridge. 'We'll wait here, I don't fancy helping you up that hill, we need an adult,' said Lindy.

They didn't have long to wait. Lindy had just finished explaining the game of Pooh Sticks when the help arrived.

Upon the arrival of the policeman, Pieter, supporting himself on Reggie's shoulder, stood to attention as best he could and saluted.

'Are you two alright? I'm PC Rowbottom at your service Lindy,' he said.

'Yes, we're fine. Thank you, Mr Rowbottom,' said Lindy. 'We could only manage to help him this far as he's very big, isn't he Reggie?'

'Yes,' mumbled Reggie. He had just recognised that the policeman was the same one who rode his bike into the car park at the golf course. Reggie turned and hid his head behind Lindy and whispered, 'That's the policeman who went to the golf club. It was his saddle bag that I put the golf balls in.'

'Shush Reggie. I shouldn't imagine he remembers you. He didn't even see you. He's probably forgotten about the balls anyway.'

In hot pursuit were two members of the newly named Home Guard. One was Roddy Butcher, the greengrocer, a large man who would have looked a lot better in a bigger uniform. He puffed as he ran down the hill.

With him was Mr Appell, the farmer, whose uniform was a better fit. He was a much healthier man owing to his hard work on the farm. They had arrived in full uniform, with their guns ready and bayonets fixed.

'Hände hoch!' said the now exhausted Mr Butcher between gasps. Pieter was the first German he had ever met. 'Hände hoch!' he shouted again.

'Yeah! Get your hands up, you dirty German,' shouted Mr Appell.

'There's no need for that,' said Lindy. 'He's surrendered to us already and has taken his gun off too. He would've given it to us, but we're too young, so he buried it on the beach.'

'Yes, you're quite right, Lindy.' said PC Rowbottom.

138

'There's no need for any fisticuffs, you can see that he's injured. I don't think he's going to fight anyone or run away.'

'That's the problem' explained Lindy, 'He can barely walk. We decided to stop and wait for you as we couldn't manage the hill. It's too steep.'

The policeman took charge. 'We must get the gun he was carrying. We don't want it to end up in the wrong hands, do we?'

'Who's we?' muttered Reggie.

'Roddy, you go back down to the beach with Reggie and bring back the gun. Now,' he turned to Pieter and in a very clear and loud voice shouted, '**Do … you … speak … English?**'

Pieter took a deep breath and spoke in an accent as would be fitting of anyone who had been to Cambridge University and had had tea with an important person.

'Yes, I do actually! Lindy and Reggie have helped me so far, but I'll need the help of someone bigger and stronger to get further up this hill, if you don't mind.'

Lindy giggled. 'Yes, he speaks English very well. We've had a lovely conversation.'

'Have you now?' said PC Rowbottom. 'I hope you haven't told him any state secrets.' He laughed at his joke.

Lindy took his statement seriously. 'I don't know any state secrets, so I couldn't have told him anyway. No, he just told us about his family.'

The party waited for Reggie and Roddy, to come back

139

with the gun. The weapon, now all covered with sand, had been opened by Roddy. 'I've taken out the bullets,' he said proudly. 'It was difficult to close again because of the grit in it.' The gun, grit and bullets were given to the policeman. 'This must be put into a safe place,' he said with authority. 'Mustn't let this get into the wrong hands, must we.'

'Who is this we?' said Reggie.

Pieter put his arms over the shoulders of the policeman and Mr Appell, and then they slowly struggled up the hill. 'We'll arrange for an ambulance to come and collect you when we get to the top.'

The walk up the steep hill was steady. Mr Appell was a strong man and he put his arm around Pieter's lower back giving him a great deal more support than had the children.

There was quite a small crowd at the top outside the cottages. Cludgy stood with Betsy and Peggy Vaughan, who had been summoned to give first aid if needed. As soon as the children saw them, they rushed over.

'I've met a German,' said Lindy, 'his name's Pieter.'

'He surrendered to us!' added Reggie.

Cludgy got a chair for Pieter, and Peggy opened her first aid bag.

'Now sit down there and let me see what's happened to your leg,' said Peggy. Very gently, she lifted his leg, cut away the material at the bottom of his trousers, and looked at the wound.

'How did this happen?' she asked.

'I was shot,' Pieter repeated his story. 'The engine of my plane got most of the bullets but I got this one.'

Cludgy brought out a bowl of warm water and Peggy bathed his leg. She cleaned off some of the sand that had entered the wound. The warm water was soothing.

'What time did this happen?' she asked.

'At about midnight. I glided and landed on the water, clambered out of the cockpit and floated. I was in the water from then until I swam in and met Lindy and Reggie this morning.'

Peggy examined Pieter's leg closely. 'The bullet hasn't hit the bone. I think it's only a flesh wound, so you're going to be fine.' She put a soft dressing over the wound, which was held in place by a further strip of bandage. She gently pulled it tight. 'Is that comfortable?' she asked.

'Thank you very much,' Pieter said, 'it feels so much better now.'

Coming around the corner was a black Bedford van, which had been converted into an ambulance. Inside were two fixed iron frames on which two stretchers could be put. Peggy helped Pieter get into the vehicle. Once seated, she carefully lifted his legs onto the stretcher that was already in place on the iron frame.

'Can we say goodbye to Pieter?' asked Lindy.

'Do you really want to?' said the ambulance man as he was about to shut the back door. 'He's a hateful

German you know! He's the wicked enemy!' His voice was raised. 'Don't you understand?'

The children didn't understand. They had met the enemy, who was not like the enemy they expected. He was not the vicious monster as shown in the papers. He was Pieter, a kind and gentle man. He was a husband, and a father, like husbands and fathers in England. He was not hateful or wicked.

'Well, if it's alright with your mum,' said the ambulance man.

'She's not my mum, she's my Cludgy!'

Cludgy nodded her head. The two children climbed into the back of the ambulance.

'Goodbye Pieter! Good luck. It was so nice to meet you,' said Lindy.

'Yes, so nice,' said Reggie as he extended his hand forward to shake Pieter's. The German pilot took it, and they shook hands warmly.

'I'm not going to forget you two, ever,' said Pieter.

'Nor us,' said Lindy as she took Pieter's other hand.

'I'll remember you forever,' added Reggie, 'forever and ever.' There was a tear in his eye.

19
The Blackberry Adventure

The skies over the Isle of Wight were very busy. Planes were heard overhead, and reports of crashed aircraft abounded throughout the month of August. The work of the RAF was unceasing.

Lindy and Reggie spent a lot of time in the shelter. They took board games to play on a small table that Arthur had made. Cludgy took her knitting.

'Is there anyone in Little Bridge you haven't made a jumper for?' asked Arthur.

Churchill made a speech in Parliament that praised the RAF. 'Never in the field of human conflict' he declared, 'was so much owed by so many to so few.'

The children had learnt lots of new skills. When they could get outside, Arthur taught them gardening and how and when to plant seeds. They helped to weed the vegetable patch and pick the produce. Lindy liked digging up the potatoes the most. 'It's like finding treasure,' she said. Arthur explained the seasons, and the children watched plants grow and turn to fruit. There were a few blackberries in the hedge around the allotments.

'In the spring these were just blossoms in the hedgerows,' explained Arthur. 'Now they've turned into blackberries. They're very good for you. If you get the chance, you must go blackberrying. They're delicious.'

'I've had blackberry jelly. Mum made some last

143

year,' said Lindy.

Early one morning, Arthur walked into the kitchen from the allotments with a handful of blackberries. 'It's going to be cloudy today. Perhaps we won't have any activities overhead, so the children might like to go blackberrying.'

'Good idea!' said Cludgy. 'I'll find them a bowl.'

'Look in the hedgerows and pick the lovely black fruit. Make sure they look like this,' Arthur said, and took a lovely big blackberry from his hand. Lindy and Reggie looked at it intently, then Arthur popped it in his mouth.

Lindy now had a wicker basket on the handlebars of her bike, and Cludgy's enamel bowl fitted in snugly.

'Take your bikes, so if you hear the siren, you can get back here quickly,' said Arthur, 'and don't go too far.'

'Yes, we know!' the children chanted.

Reggie's legs had a few more bruises and cuts: one had needed stitches at the hospital. He was very proud of that one. He had grown a great deal over the summer; his extra-long shorts were now settled at a decent height above his knees, but his bike looked smaller when his long legs pedalled.

They found a bush close by in the churchyard. Reggie rushed forward to pick a blackberry and promptly scratched his arm on the thorns.

'Ow! They bite!' he yelped.

'Are you going to make a collection of war injuries on your arms to match your legs now?' said Lindy

'Oh, Ha Ha,' Reggie said sarcastically.

Finding the fruit in the hedge rows was quite difficult. There were very few left. Everyone else had picked them. They ended up in Quarry Road, looking over the gate into a field.

'Where's the black horse that usually lives in here?' said Lindy. They leant on the gate and looked all around. Across on the other side, Reggie spotted two big masses of brambles.

'Look!' he said, 'Look over there! That big bush must be full of blackberries.'

It didn't strike either of them as to why no one else had picked blackberries from that large bush. With the bowl safely in Lindy's hands, they dropped their bikes on the ground, joyfully climbed over the gate and ran across towards the mass of brambles. They had started to pick the fruit when a large black horse's head appeared from behind it. Reggie jumped out of his skin and fell backwards into the brambles. He had never seen such a large animal close up. He was speechless.

Lindy laughed. 'Hello Shadow!' she said, walking up to the mare quietly. 'You're a pretty horse.' She nuzzled her face into Shadow's neck.

Shadow was quiet and enjoyed the attention Lindy was giving her.

But Reggie couldn't move: he was stuck in the brambles. The thorns had hooked themselves into his jumper and shorts.

'Lindy, I'm stuck!' he cried. 'I can't get up!'

Sure enough, Reggie lay on his back half covered by blackberry branches across his body and face. Lindy laughed again. 'I'll get you out. I just need to unpick you from the brambles.'

It was taking a long time for Lindy to move each individual branch, first from his face and then his clothes. 'It would help if I had something to cut them with,' she said.

'There's a penknife in my pocket' Reggie replied.

'Oh thanks. You could have said that earlier!' said Lindy. 'Can you get it?'

He tried, but one thick branch prevented him from moving his arm. 'Can you move this big one please, then I can get to my pocket?'

'Are you sure that it's in your right-hand pocket?' Lindy asked. 'I don't want to waste time and risk injury moving the wrong branch.'

'Now let me think,' Reggie said, 'I'm pretty sure.' He shut his eyes, thought and then he wriggled a little. 'No! It's in the left-hand pocket.'

'That's good. There aren't so many branches on that side, and they're thinner.' Lindy continued to move individual brambles until Reggie could move his arm and get to his pocket.

'Take great care, don't drop it,' Lindy warned, 'we'll be here for ever.'

Reggie retrieved the knife and carefully passed it to

Lindy.

Shadow was steadily munching grass nearby as Lindy performed her rescue mission but, as soon as Reggie was free, he stood up. Relieved, he shouted 'Whoopee!' and Shadow then threw her head in the air, neighed and galloped off around the field.

The children waited until Shadow was calm again, and Lindy went up to her. She stroked her neck and spoke calmly. Shadow was still.

Reggie looked left and right in case Shadow's owner was in the field. 'Right! You keep the horse occupied,' he said in a soft voice, 'and I'll pick the blackberries.'

As Lindy kept an eye on Shadow, Reggie picked like fury. He got scratched many times in his efforts to get the best fruit. He had a goal now and he was going to achieve it. Lindy managed to pick a few but was more intent on keeping Shadow calm. She would wander off and then appear behind another bush.

'Where is she, Lindy?' said Reggie, 'Where is she? I can't see her.'

'She's miles away, over the other side of the field. Calm down, Reggie. Shadow knows when you're anxious, and she becomes anxious too. Maybe I should stroke you too!' she joked.

With the bowl full of blackberries, they decided they had enough. Shadow was busy munching grass, so Lindy and Reggie slowly walked back to the gate.

Putting the bowl carefully into Lindy's basket, they

set off back to the cottage. 'Don't fall off your bike!' yelled Reggie. 'You'll spill the blackberries.'

Lindy sighed. 'It's not me that falls off bikes, it's YOU!'

Cludgy was overjoyed at the amount they had picked. 'If I can get enough sugar, I'll turn this lot into blackberry jelly. In the meantime, I have some top of the milk saved. Would you like a bowl of blackberries as a treat?'

'Oh yes please,' said Lindy and Reggie, almost in unison.

'Go and get your hands washed, while I wash the fruit,' Cludgy said. As the children turned around, Cludgy noticed the back of Reggie's jumper and trousers.

'What on earth happened to you, Reggie? You're only supposed to pick the berries, not bring the bush back too.' Reggie had small bits of bramble all over his back. There were thorns all across the back of his jumper and trousers.

'Oh. That. I fell into the bush. It was alright 'cos Lindy cut me out with my penknife.' He put his hand in his pocket and produced the knife. 'Good job it was sharp - eh?'

Cludgy took a closer look. 'You've torn your shorts and made some holes in your jumper too!'

'Have I? Oh dear! Auntie Bee's not going to be pleased with me, is she?'

'I'll mend those before you go home if you can take

148

them off. Get a towel from the bathroom and wrap it around you, then I'll get my sewing box.'

They ate their blackberries as Cludgy mended the rip in Reggie's shorts. She added a patch and sewed it neatly around the material.

'They were delicious blackberries!' said Reggie. 'What shall I do about the thorns in my jumper?'

'Sit still, I'll have a go at that. Sit on the stool and lean forwards,' Lindy instructed.

Clad only in his jumper, underwear and towel around his waist, Reggie sat on a stool whilst Lindy pulled out the thorns one by one.

Cludgy was constantly knitting, sewing or mending something or other, so was ideally suited to helping her neighbour out by mending Reggie's shorts. Many people came to her for advice, and she often took on work for others when she considered that it was too difficult for that person to fix.

She made another navy-blue skirt for Lindy for school. The previous one she had made was looking very worn out. Lindy's father found a further skirt that had belonged to her mother and sent it over for Cludgy to adapt.

'This is lovely material,' she said to Lindy, who in return gave a short smile as she was remembering her mother wearing the skirt.

'It was her favourite,' said Lindy.

It had an embroidered panel over the left hip. Cludgy

ran her fingers over the stitching.

'That is lovely, I'll keep that on your adapted skirt, if you like Lindy?' Cludgy asked. Lindy nodded as she was really pleased.

When she finally wore the skirt to school, no-one noticed or commented, except Miss Simons. 'That's a lovely skirt and such a beautiful embroidery.'

Miss Simons continued to give Lindy extra and more challenging work. There was talk, and letters to her father, regarding her going to the Grammar School. This fizzled out as no-one knew what was going to happen. Would she still be living in Little Bridge, or would she return to live with her father when the bombing had ceased? Miss Simons enjoyed coaching Lindy and she equally enjoyed the extra learning. Sometimes in class, when there was a child having difficulty with a problem, Miss Simons asked Lindy to help, in return for the extra teaching she was giving her. Lindy enjoyed this, she liked Miss Simons and thought perhaps she could be a teacher when she grew up.

20
Another Letter

Early in November when Lindy arrived home from school, there was a letter waiting for her. She didn't recognise the writing. It wasn't from her father - she had received a letter from him the day before. She opened it and, turning over the paper to the back page, she discovered that it was from Lucy, her friend from the school she had attended in Portsmouth the previous spring. Lindy had written to her with her address in Little Bridge, but up until then had received nothing. Although she had promised to write, Lindy had not expected much from her as her writing was not very good, which she'd noticed when they shared a desk.

Lucy must have taken a long time to write the letter, but her writing wasn't very clear. It was difficult sometimes to understand, as she had had to guess at some of the spellings. The address on the envelope and at the top of the letter was written very clearly in a different hand. It was an address in Dorset.

She wrote in short sentences.

'Our house was bombed,' it said. *'Mum dug out. Mum in hospital. I am in Dorset. Your Dad lifted me out of the house.'*

Lindy showed the letter to Cludgy. 'Oh, the poor little dear,' she said.

Lindy started to cry. 'What can we do, Cludgy? Oh,

151

what can we do?'

'I don't know my pet,' she said. 'With travel restrictions and the cost, we can't get over to see her, and, if we did, what could we do? Let's look at the letter again.'

Cludgy picked up the letter and the envelope.

'The address was written by someone else, so it sounds as though she is being well looked after. Her mum is in hospital, so she is alive. She has only been told the bare minimum. Maybe it's because people are too busy to explain any more. I think there is one thing we can do and that is to find out how her mother is. Once we know that, then maybe we can help her. Let's write to your father and ask him to help and find out about her mother. Do you have Lucy's full name?'

'Yes - it's Jones.'

Well, that is the first thing we shall do, and the second is to write a letter back. Use simple language so that she can read it easily herself. Your composition writing has improved immensely since last May. It looks as though her written English hasn't.'

'I used to sit next to her and help her when I was at that school. The teacher Mr Hacker was not very nice, and he used to frighten her.'

'Oh dear,' said Cludgy. 'She won't have found learning easy then.'

'No, not at all. We called him Mr Whacker because he walked around with a cane and kept hitting the desks with it.'

'Right, Lindy,' said Cludgy, 'here's the plan! You write Lucy a nice letter, full of encouragement and praise for her writing to you. Encourage her to write again. I'll write to William your dad and ask him to find out about her mother. "Operation Lucy" is what we'll call it.'

Cludgy wrote to William Elliot and told him all about Lucy's letter. She also mentioned how he had met Lucy when he carried her out of their house. Then Cludgy took the bold step of writing to Lucy's host, hoping and praying that her assumption of her being a nice person was correct.

All three letters were posted the next day and then they just had to wait.

After just a few days, the first to reply was William; he wrote one letter to both of them. There were no drawings on this letter, as he had a lot to explain. He wrote:

'I have found Mrs Jones in hospital, and yes, I remember lifting Lucy out of the house. Mrs Jones has broken her lower right leg. She had been trapped by a wall that fell when the house next door received a direct hit. Lucy and her mother had rushed to their shelter, which was under the stairs. Lucy was rescued without any injuries, as she was more to the back of the cupboard. Her mother was climbing into the cupboard when the explosion occurred, and her leg was sticking out of the door and it got crushed. The injury will heal, and Lucy is only in Dorset until her

mother is fit enough to look after her.

'They have lost everything in the explosion. I don't think Lucy had very many clothes anyway and now they are all gone. The authorities are looking for some accommodation for them when she comes out of hospital.'

'Now,' said Cludgy, 'that's something we can help with. You've grown so much since you've been here, let's have a look at the clothes you are too big for. I take it that she is smaller than you.'

'Small and skinny,' agreed Lindy, 'or maybe she's grown since I saw her last.'

'Well, we'll still send her some hand-me-downs and just hope they fit.'

The next day a letter came from Mrs Laura Golding, Lucy's host. Cludgy was right, she sounded a really kind person. She wrote:

'Thank you for your letter. I know some of the details about Lucy. I was told about her mother and her injuries. I have also agreed that when she first comes out of hospital she can come here to recuperate. I was interested to read that your Lindy had helped her at school in Portsmouth. The school doesn't sound like a nice place. The village school we have here is much smaller and dare I say a thousand times better. I am sure she will be happier here. I have also suggested to Lucy that I help her with some of her schoolwork at home, and she is overjoyed.'

154

Two days later, a letter from Lucy arrived. There was so much more written in it this time. Cludgy and Lindy immediately guessed that she had had help with the spelling. The address was written as before in a different hand. Lucy wrote:

'Thank you for your letter. I am very happy here. I have a nice bedroom. I now call Mrs Golding, Auntie Laura. She is helping me write this letter. I go to school in the village. My teacher's name is Mrs Power. She is very nice. With lots of love, Lucy.'

Lindy and Cludgy sorted through Lindy's clothes. They found various items she had grown out of: a school blouse, two vests and a thick cardigan.

'Can I send her my brown skirt I wore at Oakleigh?' asked Lindy. 'I've nearly grown out of that too.'

'Yes, a good idea. You won't be able to get in it at all if you grow as fast as you are now! It's still in very good condition.'

Cludgy finished knitting a jumper for her that she could wear at school. She had started it when Lindy first got Lucy's letter. Cludgy also bought her two pairs of knickers. They folded the clothes carefully, added a letter and wrapped the collection in strong brown paper. They tied the whole parcel securely with string, then took it to the post office and sent it to Dorset.

'Oh, I would love to see her open the parcel,' said Lindy.

'So would I' agreed Cludgy. 'That's the joy of giving.'

155

Despite all the disruptions at school Miss Simons was determined to put on a nativity play. Lindy was chosen to sing the first verse of 'Once in Royal David's City'. She knew the words, having sung it every Christmas since she could remember. As rehearsals became difficult due to the air raids, the play was becoming more like a tableau, as more and more children found it hard to learn the lines. 'There was a raid last night, I didn't have time Miss,' was the usual excuse. It was decided that the children should just move to and stand in their places and a narrator would tell the story. Lindy's voice was clear and so she was chosen to narrate the play. Reggie did not enjoy dressing up as shepherd. He saw himself as tough, and shepherds were not.

'I don't want to be a soppy shepherd,' he announced.

Miss Simons made sure he had no lines to say.

Another letter arrived from the mainland. It was for Reggie.

'Mum and Dad are coming here on Saturday!'

21
Walter and Shirley Mitchell

Ever since Auntie Bee had read the letter to Reggie, he had been dancing around the yard outside her house. Lindy was puzzled. She had thought that Reggie's father was a prisoner of war. She couldn't understand why, when the Germans were bombing the British, they had let their prisoner of war go. *Maybe he escaped,* she thought.

'I've only got to wait one day, one whole day, before I see my mum and dad.' Reggie continued dancing his strange creative dance of arms outstretched like an aeroplane, skipping, running in circles and then creating a pose of holding a gun and shooting anything and everything. 'My dad and mum are coming here!' he kept singing.

'School first!' called Auntie Bee.

Reggie's energy was unbounded. He ran, hopped and then jumped his way to school.

'I must take them to the beach and show them where we found the German pilot. I must show them the place where we played Kick the Can. I could show them the golf course.' Lindy gave him a stern look.

'Or perhaps not! I must show them the Smuggler's Grave.'

'Will you have enough time to show them everything in a weekend?' Lindy commented.

'Lindy,' Reggie said quite seriously. 'Lindy! I must

157

learn to read. Auntie Bee had to read my letter. Suppose my mum had written something very secret.'

Aware that he was stating the obvious, Lindy took a deep breath and then nonchalantly said 'Good idea, Reggie.'

'But my dad can't read,' said Reggie sadly. 'How am I going to write to him when he's away?'

The school day passed very quickly for Lindy and very slowly for Reggie. He sat there dreaming of the weekend and what he would be doing. He talked about nothing else. The whole school knew that his parents were visiting that weekend. The more he went on about the forthcoming visit, the more Lindy felt a little envious.

'I would love a visit from Daddy, but he's always too busy,' she confided to Miss Simons. 'I miss Mummy sometimes.'

Miss Simon did not know what to say.

'Be patient, Lindy, your time will come,' she said quietly. 'Now let's talk about this essay you wrote. I loved the story, and the descriptions were excellent. I could quite easily see the beach you were talking about. There are a few grammar faults to sort out.'

Going home from school was a joyous time. Lindy had received a good mark for her essay. Reggie was not interested: he was consumed with his own joy.

'But she gave me a "good", the best mark I've ever received!' insisted Lindy. 'Aren't you pleased for me?'

'Suppose so!' he said as he ran home.

158

Cludgy was very pleased about Lindy's essay. She extolled the good work to Arthur who congratulated Lindy and reminded her of the virtues of a good education.

Lindy was quiet during supper. 'Anything the matter?' asked Cludgy.

'Nothing really,' Lindy replied, 'It's just …' and she stopped in mid-sentence.

'Just what?' asked Cludgy.

'It's just that I would love my dad to come over and see me. I miss him so much.'

'Be patient, your time will come,' said Cludgy as she put her arms around Lindy's shoulders.

'That's what Miss Simons said today, but when will my time come?'

There were a few tears that evening when Lindy was in bed. Cludgy went in and stroked her hair. 'Be patient, my pet,' she kept saying. 'Be glad for Reggie. That's what he wants of you. Give him that gift of being pleased for him.'

The next morning Reggie was nowhere to be seen. Lindy called for him.

'Where's Reggie, Auntie Bee?' she asked her neighbour.

'He's gone to the bus stop on the main road to wait for his parents.'

'Best wait for him here Lindy,' said Cludgy. 'Let him greet his parents by himself.'

Reggie had cycled to the main road. He didn't cross

159

the road, but stood and watched the buses as they came from Ryde. There were a lot, almost too many for Reggie's patience. He was staring across the road as a number 1A bus had just driven off leaving its passengers on the pavement. He strained his eyes. 'Not there,' he said to himself. 'Where are they? Oh, for goodness sake, where are they?'

Just then, someone tapped on his shoulder.

'Hello son!' he said.

'Hello Reggie!' said his mother.

'Where did you come from? I've watched every bus come from Ryde. That's the way I came to the island.'

There standing in front of him together hand in hand were Walter and Shirley Mitchell.

'But we came from Southampton, so our bus came from the other direction,' said his mother.

'Hey, is this your bike?' asked his father. 'You're nearly too big for that. My goodness, haven't you grown! Let me look at you.' He stood back to admire his son.

'My Reggie! Just look at my Reggie.'

Shirley gave him a big hug. It was not one of those hugs you are given at weddings and parties from strange relatives you have not seen for ages. Reggie never understood how he was supposed to like such a hug from a stranger. But this was his mum, - he didn't want the hug to stop.

She held his hand. Reggie's dad picked up the bike and carried it on his shoulder. They walked together.

Reggie told them all about his life in Little Bridge. He repeatedly asked his father what he did in the army. 'Oh, just army things,' was his only reply.

Looking very serious, Shirley spoke to her son, 'Reggie darling, you know when you asked me about my work and I said that I simply can't tell you, remember, "Careless Talk Cost Lives", you've seen the posters. Well, it's like that, Dad can't tell you, he's not allowed to. When the war is over, he'll tell you then.'

That information added to the hero status that Reggie had for his father. *Perhaps he **is** a spy,* he thought.

Lindy had also been waiting for the family's arrival. She watched them walk down the lane towards the cottages. Walter looked very smart, dressed in his army uniform. His beret was at a jaunty angle, his battle dress fitted his slight stature. Most noticeable were his boots. They were stout and stiff, almost as if they were made out of wood. They clattered with each step. Shirley, not very tall, was wearing a red scarf around her head, which matched her warm woollen overcoat. She carried a matching red handbag. When they arrived at the cottages, Reggie introduced his parents to Auntie Bee.

'Auntie Bee, this is my mum Shirley, and my dad's name is Walter.'

'Hello Shirley. Hello Walter. So nice to meet you. I've made two extra beds up in Reggie's room for you tonight. Do come in. Shall I make some tea?'

The family disappeared into Reggie's house.

161

162

22
The Emergency

A little later there was a knock at the kitchen door. Cludgy opened it. It was Auntie Bee. 'Would Lindy like to come out and join us?'

'Lindy, would you like to join Reggie and his parents?'

'Yes please, that will be nice. Where are we going first?'

Suddenly from behind Auntie Bee Reggie appeared. 'The Smuggler's Grave!' he said. 'Come on!'

Arthur joined them. Part of his responsibilities was to check the church now and then, and this was a good opportunity. Not to miss a chance to have a walk, Texi rushed through Arthur's legs and came too. They all walked up to the graveyard, except Reggie and Texi who ran.

'He never walks slowly, he always rushes,' said Shirley, '... never still, only when he's asleep, I suppose.' It took a while for Arthur to realise that she was talking about her son Reggie and not his dog Texi. 'He hasn't changed,' she said.

'I know,' said Lindy, 'but things have changed since we got our bikes. He pedals really fast, as his bike is smaller than mine and I ride slowly. We keep up with each other.'

When they got to the gate, Reggie pulled Lindy aside and whispered to her. 'I think my dad is going to be a spy, he's doing some secret work. It's so secret that Mum said I shouldn't ask him about it.'

They stopped and looked around the graveyard. They picked their way through the gravestones which stuck out of the earth like teeth.

'Lots of people have died in Little Bridge - there are so many stones,' remarked Walter.

There were also some flat stones that Reggie jumped on. He tried to read the inscription. 'It's too faded' he said hiding the fact that his reading was not up to scratch. Lindy joined him on the stone, but she too found it difficult to decipher.

In the graveyard an old man was sitting on another flat tomb. 'Morning,' he said, 'Lovely day!'

Lindy, Reggie, Shirley and Walter replied 'Good morning' in unison.

'Hello Mr Sutterton', said Arthur.

Remaining seated, he lifted his cap from his head. 'Good morning to you, sir. Here, a few weeks ago you wouldn't have been able to stand on that stone, as it was encircled with iron railings.'

'Have they gone to salvage?' asked Shirley.

'Yep, that's right, salvage!' he announced. 'Gone to make planes or whatever. Funny sort of planes they'll make out of them straight railings!' He laughed at his joke.

'I think they melt the metal down first,' said Shirley who took his words seriously.

164

'We've come to see the Smuggler's Grave,' announced Reggie. 'This is my mum and dad.'

'How do you do,' said Mr Sutterton. 'Which smuggler's grave do you mean? We have lots. Ronnie Mumfort is over there. He died very rich. But then he didn't get caught, did he?'

'Do you mean there are lots of smugglers buried here?' asked Shirley.

'Oh yes,' he replied, 'Lots of them. Now over there's a double burial of Mr and Mrs Kettle. He died first and then she followed a couple of days later. So they got buried at the same time. They lived in a lovely house just off Quarry Lane.'

'Were they all rich?' asked Shirley.

'Oh yes, oh yes.'

'How come they didn't get caught?' Walter asked.

'Well, they were all at it, weren't they? Taxes were so high that, if they got caught, it was cheaper to pay the fine. There were always more goods to smuggle next week. They often had more than one boat, so while the customs people were catching one boat a dozen more were slipping through.'

'Where's this famous grave Reggie keeps talking about?' asked Walter.

'It's over there. It's the one with a carving of a boat on it.'

'How come he was shot? Was he a smuggler? I mean, was he guilty?' continued Walter.

'That's the mystery,' Mr Sutterton said. 'The people in the village were so angry that he was killed that they paid for the ornate gravestone.'

They stared at the gravestone and the small one at the side of another member of the same family. They found it difficult to read the inscription as the 'f's were 's's and were inscribed in old English script.

'What is the point of learning to read if they don't use the right letters?' Reggie muttered to himself.

Texi, at Reggie's instigation, chased around the church, as the adults looked at the building. Arthur explained how old it was and pointed out some important details on the masonry and stained glass. They looked at the bell tower. It was Walter who spotted it first. High up by the bell tower was a long cylinder-shaped object poking out of the roof.

'Look up there,' he said quietly to Arthur. 'I think that's an incendiary bomb.'

Arthur looked up and said 'Yes, I think you're right. You get everyone well away and I'll go back for a ladder.'

During the raid that had occurred two days before, the Luftwaffe had dropped many incendiary bombs. These were filled with highly combustible chemicals, dropped in clusters that were called 'bread-baskets'. There were different sizes, the average contained 72 incendiaries. Some had fallen into the sea, some into the grounds of the big house, but this one had landed and got stuck in the church roof. It was difficult to see as it was very close to the bell tower.

Walter didn't wait for the ladder. Below there was a monument to Mrs Dowsen shaped in the form of a cross close to the wall. Walter sprung up, put one foot on the cross, stretched up and grasped the ledge. Reaching up again he got on to the roof. He scrambled up to the bomb. 'I've got it. I'll hold it until Arthur comes back with the ladder. Get back as far as you can,' Walter instructed calmly. 'The bomb won't go off if I'm careful with it.'

Within a few minutes Arthur had returned with a ladder. He put it up against the wall of the church and climbed up. Gently Walter slid down the roof to Arthur and passed him the bomb. Now Arthur was holding the ladder and the bomb. Walter squeezed himself around Arthur on to the rung below him, took the bomb and climbed down.

Holding it as carefully as he would a baby, he descended one step at a time, until he reached the last rung.

'I'll take it now Walter,' said Shirley. 'It's alright, from my training at the factory, I know about these: they'll only explode if the end hits a hard surface, like concrete. It obviously didn't, as the roof was not hard enough. I think it may have broken a tile.'

The onlookers breathed a sigh of relief as Shirley put the bomb down well away from everyone. Arthur inspected the roof. As well as the tile that the bomb had broken, Walter had knocked a tile off and there was a hole

167

through into the church. He peered in!

'Hang on everyone, don't get too happy!' he called out. 'One's gone through the roof into the church. I can see it - it's in the gallery near the organ'.

'I'll go!' shouted Walter, 'Is the church locked?'

'No but the gallery is,' Arthur replied as he hurried down the ladder.

Walter opened the large church door. Just in front of him was a huge ornate font with a flat wooden top. 'I must get into the gallery' he said.

'I could bring in the ladder,' said Arthur.

'It'll take too long, don't worry, I'll climb up. Best get a bucket of water and a stirrup pump.'

He jumped up onto the sturdy oak lid of the font and reached up to the wooden balustrade. Pulling himself up, he cocked his leg over the top and lowered himself to the floor.

'I've found it,' he called out. The incendiary had landed on a pile of hassocks. Unfortunately, the action of Walter landing on the floor nearby caused enough vibration to knock the bomb onto the hard floor. The horrid hissing sound started and sparks began to come out of it. 'I need a bucket of water and the pump urgently!'

Reggie suddenly appeared at the church door with a bucket full of water.

'Where did you get that bucket?' asked Arthur. 'I lost that last September.'

Lindy had found some rope in Arthur's workshop in the walled garden. She ran back into the church, and tied it to the handle of the bucket. Arthur threw the other end of the rope up to Walter who hauled it up. Cludgy suddenly appeared with the stirrup pump. Reggie was already standing on the font as his father had done. He called out, 'I've got the pump Dad. Here you are. Can you reach it?' Walter hung over the gallery and gathered up the pump.

'To use the pump is really a two-man job. Can anybody get up here and help by pumping the water?' Walter said.

As quick as a flash Reggie shouted, 'I'll do it! Can anyone lift me up to my dad?'

Everyone stopped for a moment. Should they let a 10-year-old boy help to fight a fire? But there was no one else who could climb up there except Reggie, who was halfway there in any case. The hassocks were already alight!

Shirley broke the silence. 'Here, help me up on to the font and I'll lift him up. Keep down low near the floor,' she said, 'You will find more air to breathe there. Shirley was a supervisor at the factory and had been on a course on how to put out a small fire like those started by an incendiary.

Walter leant over the edge of the gallery. Holding one of Reggie's arms, he pulled him up and lifted him over the edge. Clearly and confidently, he gave instructions to

Reggie.

'Stand as far away as possible. Keep the end of the hose in the water and pump steadily.' Reggie pumped as Walter, now lying on the floor, trained the water on the flames of the small fire that the incendiary had created. A further bucket was found, filled with water ready to send upstairs. Mr Sutterton had got a message to the vicar who had run from the rectory with the keys to the gallery.

'How are you getting on?' asked the Reverend Peterson as he climbed the stairs. 'I've sent for the fire brigade.' He unlocked the padlock and slid open the door. 'Hello Reggie, how did you get up here?'

'Climbed!' he said quite proud of himself. 'This is my dad and that's my mum coming up with another bucket of water.' Shirley put down the second bucket, the hose was moved over from Reggie's bucket which was now nearly empty to Shirley's full one. Reggie started pumping again.

'Shall I take over with the pumping, Reggie?' said Reverend Peterson.

'No, it's alright, I can manage thanks.' Reggie felt quite proud of himself, and wanted that feeling to continue, so he continued to pump.

'I'm pretty certain that it's out,' Walter called out, 'but we'll make sure by keeping the area around it damp.'

'Well now,' said the vicar, 'thank you so much Mr and Mrs Mitchell, and Reggie of course. You've saved our little church, I'm eternally grateful.'

The heroic family climbed downstairs and walked out

into the sunshine to the applause of the onlookers who had gathered. The fire brigade arrived. Three men jumped down from the tender and started to unravel the hosepipe. 'Hang on,' said the leading fireman, Mr Caws, 'I'll go and see what there is to do. I can't see any smoke anywhere.' He ran into the church.

'Course you can't,' said Shirley. 'Walter has put the fire out!'

Upstairs was a soggy mess of burnt hassocks and the cylinder of the now safe incendiary bomb. 'Where's the fire?' asked Mr Caws.

'It's out!' Walter shouted from his position low on the floor.

There was a look of disappointment in Mr Caws's face.

'Apart from the three spoiled hassocks and a wet floor there doesn't appear to be much damage,' Walter reported.

'STAND DOWN!' shouted Mr Caws in his loudest leading fireman's voice, which echoed around the church. The unused hose was rolled up again. 'I need two firemen to clear up the damage.'

Mr Caws descended from the gallery and reappeared at the church door as two men rushed in and went upstairs to the site of the incident.

'There were two incendiaries,' Shirley explained to Mr Caws. 'One that got stuck in the roof and the other one that went through to the gallery and ignited. The

171

unexploded ...'

'Well, where is it?' Mr Caws was not a patient man.

'I was about to tell you,' said Shirley. She now spoke slowly and very clearly. 'The unexploded incendiary is over there, under the cherry tree. And before you ask, yes, I've kept people away from it.'

After receiving numerous pats on the back and words of praise from everyone, Arthur was finally able to get Reggie on his own.

'Reggie,' he said, 'where **did** you get that bucket from?'

'Round the back' he replied nonchalantly and honestly, 'in the far corner, I think. Somewhere over there.' He pointed vaguely to an area. 'I got the water from the outside tap.'

'That's funny, that's my favourite bucket and I always keep it by the kitchen door in case of emergencies. I wonder how it got there. AND ... how did you know it was in the corner?'

'Oh ... um ... I just spotted it lying there!'

Later that day, Arthur took Texi out for his evening walk and wandered around the church. 'I must put those tiles back on the roof as soon as possible Texi,' he told his dog. 'Now, where did Reggie say he found that bucket?'

Arthur and Texi explored the far corner of the graveyard. Arthur gave a cursory look, but Texi scrabbled in the short grass and weeds. He picked something up in his mouth.

172

'What have you got in your mouth, Texi? Come here, boy. Drop it!'

Obedient as ever, obviously expecting a game of fetch, Texi came to his master and at his feet dropped a golf ball.

23
Family

There were to be no dramas, no adventures and no excitement the next day. Lindy, Cludgy and Arthur went to church. Shirley, Walter and Reggie went for a walk together.

The church was open, but the gallery could not be used until it had been made safe. The organist, Mr Tone, could not play the organ, so the piano was dragged forward from behind the spare chairs and a cupboard full of hymn books. It was slightly out of tune and there were a few notes missing. The usual piano tuner had been called up into the army at the beginning of the conflict.

'Never mind,' said Mr Tone to the choir. 'You will just have to sing up, so the congregation are unable to hear the odd sounds the piano makes.'

Prayers of thanks were given for the deliverance of the church. 'Let us thank God' said the Reverend Peterson, 'for Mr Mitchell, who gallantly managed to climb up the outside of the building and collect an incendiary and then climb into the gallery and, with the help of Reggie and his mum, put out another incendiary, which this time was alight.'

'Reggie would have loved to have heard that,' Lindy whispered to Cludgy. She nodded.

But they were not there. Reggie took his family exploring. He told his parents all about the smugglers, the

174

cycle ride they took and the other beach with the smelly bog. Slightly embarrassed, he told them about the goat. They thought it hilarious. Reggie was so happy with his mum and dad. 'Isn't this a lovely day?' he said for the umpteenth time.

'Yes Reggie, it is lovely,' said his mother.

They walked into Ryde. Reggie showed them the pier and where he had arrived on the island. He told them all about Miss Vaughan, who had met him and all the other children at the end of the pier. 'They checked us for nits,' he said. 'I didn't have any.'

'I should hope not,' said Shirley in a slightly indignant manner.

On the way back they passed the golf course. 'That's the golf course,' he said and then stopped himself, as he was not sure what the reaction would be if he told them about the stolen golf balls. Reggie did however tell his parents at great length all about Pieter.

They walked down the long lane to the beach, and Reggie showed them how he was able to jump over the stream. He managed four jumps before it spread out so wide, as the tide was out, that he landed with both feet in the water.

'Reggie! You must take care,' Shirley said. 'You've got wet feet.'

'I know, it happens all the time. They'll dry. When we get back for lunch, I'll take them off, stuff them with newspaper and put them near the fire.'

175

Walter and Shirley were amazed at Reggie's ingenuity. 'You've picked up some good habits while you've been here,' Shirley remarked.

They climbed the hill back up to the cottage, where Auntie Bee had made them a lovely lunch. After they had eaten, they took a short rest. Shirley made sure that her bag was packed, and that the bedroom was in order. They took a further short walk to where the game of Kick the Can was played. 'We had to use a box for the can, as it had gone to salvage,' Reggie explained.

Walter checked his watch. 'We must be on our way soon, I have to check in at 22 hundred hours,' he said.

'What time?' asked Reggie.

'That's ten o'clock tonight,' he said, 'it's army talk.'

Back at the cottage, they picked up their bags ready to leave. They made their goodbyes to Betsy Brown, who had made them some sandwiches for the journey.

'Thank you so much for looking after Reggie for us,' Shirley said. 'One day this war will be over, and we can come over for a holiday.' She turned to her son and cuddled him tightly, not wanting to let go.

'Reggie,' said his father, 'take your bike with you when we go to the bus. Then you can cycle back and it won't take long for you to get home.'

The family walked up the road together. Shirley held her bag in one hand and Reggie's hand with the other. His father picked up his bag with one hand and lifted the bike over his other shoulder.

176

Betsy shed a tear as she watched the three disappear around the corner.

At the bottom of Little Bridge Hill, a bus was already waiting at the stop. 'No time for long goodbyes,' said Walter to his son, as he crossed the road. Shirley did manage to give Reggie a quick kiss before she too ran across to join her husband. 'Be good Reggie.' 'And be clever,' butted in his father. 'I love you darling,' his mother added. Reggie was now alone with his bike on the other side.

The bus moved off up the hill, as Reggie's mum and dad waved out of the upstairs back window. All alone now, he stood still waving until he couldn't see the bus anymore.

Reggie had to admit to himself that he was crying. However, it wasn't long before the old Reggie returned. He mounted his bike, set off and became an RAF fighter pilot flying a Spitfire, firing a gun at the Germans.

'Daca daca daca daca!' he shouted as he fired his gun. Reggie 'the brave Reggie' had returned and he cycled as fast as he could back to the cottages. As he passed the church, he fired his last bullets, did a sharp turn in to the path at the side of the houses, skidded his back tyre and landed his bike at Cludgy's kitchen door.

'Come in,' Arthur called out. 'No need to knock: we heard you coming.'

Seated at the table were Cludgy, Arthur, Lindy and Auntie Bee, his island family.

'Well! I got them safely onto the bus to Cowes,' he announced.

'Do you want a drink Reggie?' asked Cludgy.

'Yes please! I'm gasping!' said Reggie, acting as if he had cycled miles, instead of the short distance from the bus stop.

Reggie drank his whole glass of water in one. He was still in the character of being a pilot drinking beer after landing his Spitfire.

'My, my, you were thirsty' said Auntie Bee.

There was a feeling of sensitivity for Reggie, as he had just said goodbye to his parents who he loved so much. The room was silent - no one knew what to say.

'It was lovely to meet your parents,' said Betsy.

'Yes, it was,' agreed Cludgy.

'What a brave man! Climbing up the church wall as he did to deal with an unexploded incendiary,' Arthur chipped in. 'Your mum, dad and you made quite a little team when you put out the fire in the gallery.'

For Lindy, things didn't quite add up. 'Reggie,' she asked, 'you said that your dad was a prisoner? Where was he a prisoner? Did he escape?'

'No, they let him out so he could join the army and go on secret missions.'

Lindy was more confused. 'What was the name of the prison?'

'The Scrubs,' replied Reggie.

Lindy was more confused than ever, as that didn't

sound German at all, and why were the Germans letting him out of a prisoner of war camp to come home and fight against them?

In a flash Arthur suddenly said. 'Where was this prison called 'The Scrubs'?'.

'Wormwood,' said Reggie.

'And where is Wormwood?' continued Arthur.

'London,' said Reggie innocently. He was confused as to why no one had understood where it was.

'What was he doing before he was a prisoner in the Scrubs?' asked Lindy.

'He was a burglar!' he announced. There was a pause. Cludgy sniggered but quickly covered her mouth.

'He was very good at it,' Reggie continued, 'He used to climb up the outside of houses and get in the very top windows!' Reggie was very proud of his father's ability.

'He wasn't that good,' Arthur whispered to Cludgy. 'He got caught.'

Betsy was silent. Perhaps a little later she would go through the rights and wrongs of climbing up the outside of buildings and stealing.

Once more the room was silent. Again, no one knew what to say. Cludgy, Arthur, Betsy and Lindy all understood that he had been a thief. Reggie worshipped his father who could climb up walls unaided. To him he was his hero.

Arthur broke the silence. 'So now he's going to Scotland, is that right?'

179

'Yes, I think so. He's going to do some special training somewhere up north,' said Reggie. 'Scotland is in the north, isn't it?'

'Yes, it is,' said Arthur. 'He has obviously been spotted for his ability to climb up the outside of buildings.'

Reggie's island family had just spent an enjoyable weekend with Walter and Shirley. They all liked Walter. No one wanted to spoil Reggie's happiness or his pride in his parents.

24
Preparing for Christmas

After the excitement of Reggie's visitors, life settled down for the preparation for Christmas. There were very few goods to buy in the shops as presents. No toys were being made, and food was in short supply. There were no exotic fruits from abroad. No bananas or oranges.

Reggie called in just as Lindy was finishing her breakfast. The conversation soon turned towards Christmas. They reminisced about the previous year. They talked about turkey dinners with Christmas Pudding, about presents stuffed into socks left by Father Christmas, and about finding parcels around the tree.

'I don't know what I can give my daddy for Christmas,' said Lindy.

'Neither do I,' said Reggie, 'My dad that is, not yours.'

'There's nothing to buy in the shops, and I've no money anyway.'

'No, there's nothing' repeated Reggie.

'Perhaps we could make them something?' suggested Cludgy. 'Your dad would be very pleased to see how your writing has improved,' she said to Lindy. She turned to Reggie, 'And you like drawing, so you could make him a Christmas card.'

'I'm sure you can use some of the crayons from school,' Lindy said.

'Yeah, I like that idea,' said Reggie. 'What are you

181

going to give your dad, Lindy?

'I've been thinking about that. Mummy used to write me long letters when I was at Oakleigh.'

'But you write him long letters now, so how is that different and special for Christmas?'

'Mummy used to make up stories about the animals that lived near our home. She used to give them names and send them on adventures. I'm going to write a story about Goaty-Goaty and the chickens.'

'That's a good idea. He'll like that, I'm sure,' Cludgy smiled. 'Will you read the story to us before you send it, please?'

'Of course, I will. I'm going to make it into a book with a cardboard cover. I can use a Shredded Wheat packet for the back and front, and then sew in the pages like a real book. I'm not quite sure how to do that bit.'

'I can help you there,' said Cludgy.

'It'll look a bit daft,' said Reggie, 'with a Shredded Wheat on the cover of a book about a goat and six chickens, won't it?'

'I've thought of that,' Lindy reassured him, 'I'll get a piece of paper and write on the title of the book and stick it onto the cardboard to cover up the Shredded Wheat words.'

'What can I get my mum?' asked Reggie.

They sat quietly and thought.

'Why don't you put your coats on and get a bit of fresh air before you start work,' Cludgy said. 'You never know, you may get an idea outside.'

They took a walk down to the beach. As they walked along the shoreline, Reggie picked up flat stones and skimmed them into the sea. 'Did you see that? I did three skims!' he said, doing one of his dances with his arms in the air. 'I'm a champion!' he shouted.

Lindy picked up a stone and looked at it. 'Reggie, I've got it! I've got an idea!' she shouted. 'You could paint a picture on one of these and it then becomes a paperweight.'

'A what?'

'A paperweight,' said Lindy. 'You put it on top of your papers on your desk or table, so they don't blow away.'

'But mum doesn't have papers that need to have a stone put on them, so they don't blow away.'

'Ahh! But she will now you've become so good at writing. She'll have lots of your letters to put under the paperweight you're going to give her for Christmas.' This was yet another hint from Lindy to encourage Reggie to write more.

They looked for a suitable stone. Reggie picked up the largest one in front of him.

'You can't send that in the post - it'll cost a fortune in stamps,' she said. 'You'll have to find a smaller one. The stones are flat here, big enough to paint a picture on. Look for a small flat stone.'

It took a while to choose a suitable stone that was flat enough and big enough on which a picture could be painted but light enough to go in the post.

A stone was chosen. 'Is this small and light enough?' asked Reggie.

Lindy held it in her hand, shut her eyes and concentrated on the weight. 'Yes, this is fine! Hey, it looks like a diamond. It's shaped like the Isle of Wight.'

The two children rushed up the hill and back to the cottages. They ran into Cludgy's kitchen. 'We know what we're going to make for my mum and dad, and for Lindy's dad!' Reggie blurted out.

'We'll have to borrow some crayons, paints and glue from school,' Lindy continued, 'and can I have the Shredded Wheat package when you've finished with it, please?'

'No,' said Cludgy. The children look downhearted.

'Why?' they asked.

'Because I've all you need here. I've a box of crayons and my old paints will be fine. I can make glue out of flour and water. Now what else do you need?'

'We need paper to write a story on and Reggie needs paper to make a Christmas card for his dad.'

'Leave the problem of paper with me, I'll see what I can find. Now, it's time you went home Reggie, it's getting dark, and you need to eat your tea before the siren goes.'

The skies were busy at night; the air raid siren recorded its 257th air raid warning on the 15th of November. Although cold, Lindy and Reggie were used to the shelters, and settled down to sleep as soon as they got into their bunks.

A couple of weeks after Walter and Shirley had left, Betsy and Reggie were in the shelter together. There were planes flying overhead now and then, but on the whole it was quiet. This was her opportunity to have a chat with Reggie.

'Your Dad was so clever climbing up the side of the church, wasn't he?' Auntie Bee said.

'Yeah, not half,' replied Reggie. 'He's so fast as well.'

'I liked them very much you know,' Auntie Bee continued.

'I love them too, and I miss them. I wish we could all live together like we used to in Portsmouth. We used to have such fun. When I played football with my mate and we lost a ball over someone's wall, I'd call my dad, and he'd climb over and get it for us.'

'That was nice of him.'

'Yeah, he's nice like that.'

'I think he is very nice, and I admire him for his ability to climb up walls.' Auntie Bee was trying to get back to her point.

Reggie sat still and thought for a while. He hadn't understood meaning of the word 'admire'.

'Does admire mean like?'

'And respect.'

'Yeah, I admire him too,' Reggie said.

Auntie Bee continued, 'When he had climbed up those walls to the top of houses what did he do then?'

'I dunno!' Reggie shrugged his shoulders.

Betsy was confused: maybe he didn't understand that his father stole things from houses. She decided to change the subject a little.

'You know it's wrong to take things from other people, don't you Reggie?'

'Yeah, I know. When the vicar came to school, he told us about the ten commandments.'

'Yes, that's right, - "Thou shalt not steal". If someone took your bike for example, would you be upset, Reggie?'

'Not 'alf!' said Reggie. He looked at Auntie Bee incredulously. 'I love my bike.'

'So, you understand that taking things from other people or places without permission is wrong and you mustn't do it.'

'You mean like the golf balls!'

'Golf balls? What are you talking about?'

'Oh nothing! … err … I found a golf ball and gave it to a man who was crossing the lane.' Reggie was relieved he could speak the truth.

'That was nice of you!'

'Yeah, Lindy made me.'

The all clear was sounded. Auntie Bee and Reggie were both very glad that the conversation had concluded.

They picked up their blankets and walked back into the house.

'Golf balls?' said Auntie Bee. Reggie chose not to hear that last comment. He ran ahead wanting to get to

186

his bedroom, so he didn't have to continue this difficult conversation. He shut the door quickly and jumped into bed, pulled the covers over him, and closed his eyes to appear as if he had fallen promptly asleep!

'Golf balls?' muttered Auntie Bee, as she made her way to bed.

25

Bartering at the Big House

The next morning Betsy and Cludgy were sitting in the kitchen having a cup of very weak tea.

'Sorry about the tea! It has very little flavour,' said Cludgy, 'I've run out and I've tried to squeeze another couple of cups out of this pot that we had at breakfast.'

'It's wet, warm and OK.' Betsy shut her eyes to concentrate. 'I think I can just about manage to get a weak tea flavour out of it,' she said.

They laughed.

'I spoke to Reggie last night about his father being a burglar,' said Betsy.

'Oh, did you?'

'Well, I did but not in so many words. The word burglar didn't come into the conversation.'

'Go on!'

'We spoke about taking other people's belongings without asking. Like someone taking his bike from him. He knew the eighth commandment; he had learnt it at school.' She took a sip of her tea. 'Do you know I don't think he understood that his father was a thief? He spoke about his ability to climb up the outside of houses, but he didn't know what he did when he got there!'

The two women laughed again.

'I do like coming around here. We always seem to end up laughing,' said Betsy. 'Funnily enough he did mention something that puzzled me. He talked about golf balls.'

'Golf balls?' yelled Cludgy.

The two women suddenly looked at each other as it dawned on them both at the same time.

'Golf balls!' they repeated together. Cludgy suddenly said 'Do you think that he's responsible for …?'

'… for the theft of the golf balls from the golf club?' Betsy butted in.

They sat still, both had their elbows on the table and their heads in their hands!

'I wonder what happened to the balls?' said Cludgy.

'I don't know!' replied Betsy.

They both thought for a minute. Then Cludgy said, 'Do we really want to know what happened to the golf balls when there's a war on? We're drinking tea that has little or no flavour and we're spending bitterly cold nights outside in our gardens in corrugated iron shelters.'

'Freezing cold!' said Betsy. 'We're making meals out of practically nothing as there's nothing in the shops. We're making clothes from old clothes and knitting jumpers from old jumpers. Surely we're too busy to worry about a few golf balls belonging to a few wealthy people.'

'Shall we just forget about it?' suggested Cludgy.

'Yes, good idea. I think Reggie understands now that taking something from someone is wrong.'

'Let's hope so,' Cludgy agreed. 'Now I must find some paper. Did Reggie tell you that they're making

189

presents for their parents? I've got paints, crayons and glue. Oh … err… and a box of Shredded Wheat!'

'Shredded Wheat?' said Betsy totally bemused.

'Yes, it's for the cover of Lindy's book. She's writing a story for her father. I'm now looking for some clean white paper to go in between the Shredded Wheat cover on which she can write her story. Her idea is that she sews it into a cardboard cover.'

'Won't it look a bit silly with a picture of Shredded Wheat on the cover?'

'Ah yes, but I've thought of that. I can make glue out of flour and water, and she can stick a cover over it with the clean white paper that I've yet to find.'

'I can help there,' said Betsy. 'I was given a pad of writing paper two Christmases ago. I don't write many letters myself. She can have that. It's not white though, it's a pale shade of pink.'

'Oh, thank you. I'm sure it being pink won't matter, although Reggie's Christmas card might look a bit unseasonal with a pink background.'

They finished drinking their tea and put their cups down.

'What about Sir?' Betsy suggested. 'I mean Mr Bovington-Brown who lives in the Quays. He has an office there.'

'So he does. What a good idea. I'll pop around there later on and ask,' replied Cludgy.

After lunch that day, Cludgy walked to the big house,

190

with Texi firmly on a lead. As she approached the front door, she wondered whether she shouldn't have gone to the servants' entry around the back. She didn't work there anymore so she wasn't a servant, she mused, so she confidently pulled the large knob and heard it ring deep in the house.

'I'll get it!' came a disembodied voice from inside.

The door opened and there was Mr Bovington-Brown.

'Who is it?' called a female voice.

'It's Cludgy!' said Mr Bovington-Brown. 'Good morning, Cludgy - have you come back to work for me?' he laughed haughtily at his joke.

'No sir,' replied Cludgy, 'I've come begging.'

'Come in, come in and bring Texi with you. He and I are well acquainted. Rufus and I often meet up on our walks.' Rufus was a very old Irish Wolf Hound who walked very slowly. Texi loved running rings around him. As they stepped into the large hall, Rufus gave two weak barks to assert his authority as being a guard dog.

'Now now Rufus,' said Mr Bovington-Brown, 'it's only Texi and Cludgy.'

Rufus laid his head back on the rug in front of the fire, asserting his place in the room. Mr Bovington-Brown stepped over him. 'Do take a seat'. Texi thought that instruction was meant for him, jumped up on the sofa and settled down.

'So sorry. Texi - you naughty boy, get down at once.'

191

Texi didn't, and just made himself more comfortable by turning three times in a circle before he flopped down.

'Leave him there, he looks so comfortable,' said Mr. Bovington-Brown.

Cludgy sat on the end of the sofa, ready to grab Texi if he misbehaved. His wife, Sarah was already seated doing some embroidery. 'Shall I order some tea, Henry? I'm sure Cludgy would like some. I would offer you coffee, but we just can't get any. We had some boys in from the private school in Ryde collecting acorns in our grounds. They said it was to make coffee.'

'Darling, you have to admit it was foul!' said Mr Bovington-Brown.

'Yes, they made some at school and they gave some to us to try. I carefully followed the instructions, but it wasn't that nice,' said Sarah, 'and it tasted nothing like coffee at all.'

'It was absolutely awful darling!' he repeated as he pulled a face.

'So anyway, it's only tea that I can give you,' offered Sarah.

'Oh no thank you, I've only just had a cup with my lunch,' she replied, thinking to herself, that she would have liked to take home the teaspoonful of dry tea leaves instead for Arthur and Lindy.

'How can we help you?' said Sarah.

'It's about the children,' Cludgy tentatively said.

'They are not ill, I hope.'

'No, no, far from it,' said Cludgy, 'they are as fit as fleas. They're making presents for their parents to send home for Christmas and I'm short of one thing.'

'What are they making?' Sarah put down her needlework.

Lindy is writing a story for her father, and Reggie is painting a stone as a paperweight for his mother and making a Christmas card for his father.'

'I think I've met Reggie. We see him in church with Betsy of course,' said Henry, 'but we've also met in the lane: he handed me back a golf ball last summer. Nice young chap!'

'And then of course Henry, it was Reggie and his parents who saved our church from burning down!' Sarah reminded him. 'What a lovely family! Such nice people.'

'Oh yes. Reggie's father climbed up the outside of the church and retrieved the incendiary bomb. What a good chap. His name escapes me, what is it?' Mr Bovington-Brown went on.

'Who?' Cludgy was a little rattled. She was not used to asking for favours or begging. She had come prepared with her request. She had rehearsed what she was going to say as she walked from the cottage to the big house and now, they were talking about the fire. 'Reggie's father's name is Walter, and his mother is Shirley,' she spluttered.

'What a lovely family, such nice people,' repeated Mr Bovington-Brown. 'I often see young Reggie in church.

193

Didn't see him with his parents though.'

'No, they went for a walk together that day,' said Cludgy. The conversation was getting further and further away from what she had called for. 'It's for Reggie that I'm here. He needs some white card to make the Christmas card, and I was wondering if you had some in your office that he could have.'

'For such a nice honest young boy, anything,' he said. He turned to his wife. 'You know your way around my secretary's office better than I do, will you help here, Sarah?'

'Of course I will, come with me Cludgy,' said Sarah. 'Don't disturb Texi, he looks so comfortable.'

'Be as generous as you like!' Henry called out as they walked through the door. 'Such a nice family.'

Cludgy was flattered that she was being treated as a guest, almost an equal, a relationship far removed from her being a servant in the house.

They entered the office, a room she hardly went into when she worked there. All communications with the lady of the house took place in the sitting room, where she would sit on an upright dining chair, while Sarah Bovington-Brown would sit on the sofa, her papers scattered all around her. Here they would discuss menus and organisation of the many guests that would come and spend weekends with the Bovington-Browns.

She looked around the room. The typewriter was idle and covered in dust. Sarah ran her finger across the dusty desk. 'I just can't get any staff these days. You retired and then Rosemary left me to be a land girl. Young Joseph who used to work for you is still with us, he's a great help with Isobel the goat. I don't think he will be called up because of his limp. He's had that all his life. Cheerful chap! Can't find anyone else, they can all get more money making munitions or aeroplane parts. I've had to learn how to cook!'

'Aeroplane parts! That's what Shirley does,' said Cludgy.

'Shirley? Shirley who?'

'Reggie's mother!'

Sarah opened a drawer in the desk and there was a pile of beautiful white card. Cludgy's face lit up. 'How much do you want?' asked Sarah.

'One sheet will do' replied Cludgy, not wanting to appear greedy.

'Take two just in case he makes a mistake and wants to start again.'

'Thank you so much, that's perfect.' Just then Cludgy spotted a pot of glue on top of the sideboard. 'Oh, you have some glue!'

'Do you want some?' Sarah picked up the pot and tried to turn the lid. It wouldn't budge, it was firmly stuck on. 'I'm afraid it's a bit old. I can't seem to get the lid off. You're welcome to it. Here, do take the glue brush too. If you can get into the pot, you'll need that,' she laughed.

'Arthur will find a way of getting the lid off,' said

Cludgy, knowing that warm water would soften the glue and the lid could then be eased off.

'Thank you so much. Homemade glue made of flour and water can go mouldy with time and this won't. It's so much better.'

'Is there anything else I can help you with?' Sarah asked.

'Is there anything else I can do for you?' Cludgy replied, 'I've very little in my store cupboard to swap.'

'I need some mending done. My mother made sure that I could do embroidery, but she didn't teach me how to mend clothes. "That's for the servants to do, not respectable young ladies!" she would tell me. Are you short of anything?'

'Well, now you should mention it I am a little short of tea! It's so difficult to get hold of it.'

'Yes, I can give you some tea!'

'And I can do some mending for you in return.'

Cludgy returned home carrying a borrowed shopping basket in one hand and holding Texi's lead in the other. He was behaving very well for once. In the basket were two of Sarah's dresses, two pieces of white card, a pot of glue, glue brush and a small bag of tea.

Arthur was sitting at the kitchen table when Cludgy walked in.

'Successful trip?' he asked as he spotted her with the basket.

'Not half!' she replied, imitating Reggie.

26
Making Christmas

After school, and at the weekend, Reggie came round to where Cludgy had set up a workplace on the dining room table. She had covered the table with old newspaper, taking care not to allow horrific pictures of the results of bombing to be visible, that it seemed appeared in every paper, every day.

She had brought her old paint box down, and was able to get three more pots of paint: yellow, blue and red.

'With these three colours you can mix them to create any colour you like,' she explained. 'Look, I'll show you.'

The children sat quietly and watched as Cludgy mixed the colours. They were most amazed when the yellow and blue were mixed. 'Wow! It's green!' said Reggie in surprise.

Their Studio, the name thought up by Cludgy, was a hive of industry for the next few days. Cludgy was always there to give help with anything. Reggie was anxious to get going with the paints, but Cludgy had to stop him from using the precious white card immediately.

'It took a great deal of trouble to get that,' she said, 'I'm not sure I can get any more. Plan out your picture on rough paper first and then copy it onto the white card.' She ironed some sheets of paper that had wrapped some clothes that Lindy's father had sent from Portsmouth when the weather turned cold. 'I know it's brown, but

197

you can use it to practise on, saving your best work for the card,' she advised, adding, 'why not draw something first and then colour it with the paints.' There were paints at school, but they never had the variety of colours that Cludgy had found, nor did they have such individual help that she was giving.

Lindy made a rough copy of her story. 'There, that's finished. I must correct it and write it out again and put it into the book.'

'Will you tell us the story?' Reggie asked.

'Oh yes do,' shouted Cludgy from the kitchen.

'OK, if you really want me to,' said Lindy slightly embarrassed, but very flattered.

'Do you want me to help you with spellings and punctuation?' Cludgy offered.

'Yes, that's a good idea,' Lindy replied.

Lindy cleared her throat and picked up the paper on which she had written the story. She began, *'Once upon a time, there was a beautiful goat called Isabel, who lived in a field in Little Bridge. She was a lonely goat who had no goat friends. Her only friends were the six white chickens, who lived in the field next door. They cackled too much, and never listened to what Isabel was saying. One day, two naughty children brought home a goat, who they thought was missing.'*

Here Lindy stopped reading. 'That bit is not really true as we brought home a lady goat.'

'I don't think that matters at all,' said Cludgy, 'as it's

198

all not true in any case!'

Lindy sighed and then continued. '*He was put in a field nearby, and Isabel and Mr Goaty fell in love. The monks came, and took Mr Goaty home, and Isabel was sad. The six chickens tried to comfort her, but Isabel cried.*

'*That night, Mr Goaty came and visited her, and she was happy. The chickens didn't see him, as they were in their hen house.*

'*He visited many times, and they decided, to get married. So, after one very early morning visit, Mr Goaty was found by Isabel's owner, Henry Bovington-Brown. 'Hello Mr Goaty,' he said, 'what are you doing here?'*

'*Mr Bovington Brown had worked with goats, for many, many, years and somehow, through magic, was able to understand that Isabel, and Mr Goaty, wanted to get married.*

'*So, Mr Goaty, Isabel, and Mr Bovington Brown went to see the vicar, Shadow, the black horse, he agreed to marry them. On the following Saturday Isabel, decorated with flower around her neck, walked into Little Bridge Church, followed by six white chickens as bridesmaid paraded down the aisle, to meet up with Mr Goaty, and they were married.*

'*The monks agreed, that they should live together, in Mr Bovington-Brown's field, and they all lived happily ever after.*'

Cludgy and Reggie clapped. Lindy got up and bowed!

Cludgy took the rough script. 'There are a couple of

spelling mistakes, here and here, and also I suggest you put a full stop there. There are a lot of commas, why do you use so many commas, Lindy?'

'I don't really know. So, I can take a breath when reading it.'

'Well, there are rather a lot. Shall we take some out?'

'You're going to have to design a cover, Lindy,' said Reggie.

'Oh yes, I haven't given that much thought.'

'Let's get the writing done first,' said Cludgy wisely, 'and think about that later.'

'Cludgy, you know some books have a page that they dedicate the book to.'

'Yes, that's right they do. Do you want to add one?'

'I want to dedicate it to Mummy. She used to write stories like this in her letters she sent to me when I was at Oakleigh in Brighton.'

'What a lovely idea!' said Cludgy. 'Do you know what to write?'

'No, not really.'

'May I suggest something?'

'Yes please.'

'I suggest: "This book is dedicated to my mummy who used to write silly and funny animal stories in her letters to me at boarding school."'

'That's lovely,' said Lindy. 'I think she would like my story, don't you?'

'Yes I think she would,' Cludgy agreed.

Reggie picked up his stone and pondered where to start. He picked up a paint brush from the box. Instead of long bristles, it had short stubble at the end. 'Did you buy this like that?' asked Reggie.

'No, my sister cut it, when she was five. She said she had given it a haircut!'

'Why didn't you throw it away?'

'I thought it might be useful one day,' Cludgy said.

Reggie looked at it, and with a stabbing movement he hit the paper. Cludgy looked closely at what was happening when he stabbed the paper.

'I know!' shouted Cludgy with joy. 'What would happen if you put paint on the end of the brush before you stabbed it on the paper. Go on - try it out Reggie.'

He dipped it in the red paint and stabbed it onto the paper. There appeared in front of him, lots of red dots. 'I could use another colour to make a pattern!' he said excitedly.

'Now that would be great on your stone!' suggested Cludgy. 'You could make a lovely pattern with dots of different colours.'

'I thought that art had to look like something, like a person or a view.'

'Oh no, you can do anything with anything. You can use paint to make a picture, you could use shells or stones from the beach to make a pattern.'

'What fun!' said Lindy.

Reggie picked up his stone and ran his fingers over its

201

shape. Then he chose only three colours to use. He made a start with the mutilated paint brush.

'That's lovely, well done, Reggie,' said Cludgy looking over his shoulder at his work, 'I knew that brush would be useful one day!'

Reggie had just finished his design on his stone when Cludgy stopped him. Auntie Bee was calling him for lunch. 'What a masterpiece of abstract design.'

Reggie didn't quite understand what an abstract design was, but appreciated the praise, nonetheless.

The two children went straight back into the Studio after lunch and started work again. Cludgy joined them and corrected Lindy's story. Reggie was now doing rough copies of his Christmas card for his dad and Lindy was trying to design a cover for her book. It was obvious that Reggie was much better at drawing than Lindy.

'Oh Cludgy, I'm useless. I'm no good at this, nothing looks at all like a goat or a chicken!'

'No, you're not useless' Cludgy assured her. 'You are good at writing stories. Reggie is better at drawing, that's all. Now I've an idea. Let's see if we can find a picture of a goat and one of a chicken that you can trace. There are some books stored in your room - maybe there's one that has some pictures of farmyard animals.'

She rushed upstairs to her room and found the box of books. 'Why have you got books stored in your house?' asked Lindy.

'They were left over from a jumble sale we did for the

church. These books were too good to throw away, so I've given them a home, until the next jumble sale.'

Mr Goaty came to life quite quickly. Under the letter "G" in a book about the alphabet was a goat. Disappointingly, in the same book "C" had a cow on the page, not a chicken. She lifted each book out of the box and flicked through them. She must have scoured 50 books, before she found one about a farmyard in it with some chickens. Unfortunately, they were rather small. She took the books down to Cludgy.

'The goat is fine: he will fit on the cover easily, but the chickens are too small,' said Lindy

'That's no problem, no problem at all,' Cludgy said, looking closely at the pictures. The chickens can be in the background. Things always look smaller the further back they are.'

Cludgy found some greaseproof paper she used for her cakes. She then explained to Lindy how to trace the pictures from the book. She covered the outline of the drawing on the back with pencil and transferred the drawing onto the paper she was going to use for the cover. Carefully she painted her design and added the title.

Cludgy, knowing that the glue would be needed, carefully put the pot in a bowl of warm water. They left it for a while until the whole pot was warm and Arthur then carefully eased the lid open. Lindy continued to add some coloured paints to her artwork. 'What do you think,

Cludgy?' she asked.

'My, my. That's looks quite good,' said Cludgy. 'Now we need to leave that to dry before we stick it to the cereal pack cover.'

After supper, Lindy, carefully using the glue brush, spread glue evenly over the back of her picture. Cludgy held the cardboard cover as Lindy carefully placed it. She pressed it down.

'There, that looks good!' Lindy said.

It was Arthur's turn to help now. With his bradawl and hammer he made evenly spaced little holes in the cover and the paper on which Lindy had written the story. Using some embroidery silk, she carefully stitched the book to the cover.

Cludgy helped them pack up the presents: the hardest to do was the stone. She had found some tissue paper, but that wasn't robust enough, so she wrapped it in some old sacking as well. 'Now the brown paper and string,' Cludgy sighed. The parcel was round and difficult for the string to stay in one place.

Reggie was despondent! 'Won't we be able to send it?' he said.

'Cludgy will think of something,' said Cludgy. 'Where are the remains of the Shredded Wheat package?' Using the glue and strips from the side of the packet, Cludgy made a box.

'Oh, aren't you clever!' said Reggie.

'Thank you, Reggie, that's nice of you to say so!'

It was easy now to wrap up the parcel with its precious contents of a painted beach stone. They took the three parcels to the post office and handed them over the counter.

'That one is for my dad,' said Lindy told the post mistress.

'And those two are for my dad and mum,' continued Reggie.

It was slightly sad saying goodbye to all that hard work.

Now the children didn't know what to do with themselves after their spell in the Studio. They went around the woods and picked holly and ivy to decorate their homes. Christmas seemed ages away, both children still wanted the magic of the special day, but both missed their parents.

'We'll do our best to make the day joyful and full of fun,' said Cludgy to Betsy.

27
Joy!

The Isle of Wight was a closed area during the war, and to travel to the island needed authorisation from the Isle of Wight Constabulary. William applied to the assistant chief constable's office in Fairlee Road in Newport, Isle of Wight, early in December to visit the island, the purpose was to see his daughter. He wanted to visit Lindy on Christmas Day: however this date had to fit in with leave from the fire service, other firemen wanting time off as well as the likelihood of raids. There had been attacks on Portsmouth on the 5th and 6th of December, when he applied, and there was a heightened need to have a full complement of firemen on duty throughout. William had not heard whether the fire service would allow him to have time off, or that the assistant chief constable of the Hampshire Joint Police Force would give him permission to travel across the Solent to the Island.

The delivery of mail had been spasmodic throughout December. There were a lot of letters and cards going to relatives and friends. Some never made their destination for many reasons, mainly caused by 'Enemy Action'. William watched the mail arrive every day. He had had a letter from Lindy but had heard nothing from the Hampshire Joint Police Force, so on the 20th of December, he applied again. On Christmas Eve, following three busy days of raids, he received his official letter giving him permission to visit the Isle of Wight. It stated that he could choose a time from within next seven days. This permission would expire on the 1st of January, 1941. He showed the letter to his section commander Geoff Knight, who knew he could not release him for the whole seven days. He was reluctant to give him leave, as the wealthy Ronald Demby-Smythe had managed to get time off. Geoff was one man down already.

'I only want a day or two, please,' William pleaded, 'I do need to see Lindy - I've not seen her since I put her on the ferry last May.'

'Alright,' Geoff said, 'what about Boxing Day? There are no boats to the island on Christmas Day anyway. Sorry it's just one day, but we are so short of men at the moment, Harry has asked for leave as well. And who knows what Hitler has planned for us over the Christmas period.'

'That's the day after tomorrow!' William said. 'How am I going to let them know I'm coming?'

'There must be some official who you could telephone who would get a message to her.'

William had a stroke of genius. 'The vicar! That's who!' he exclaimed.

William had his leave granted, and his permission letter was safely stowed in his pocket. Nothing was going to stop him now.

Christmas Day for Lindy, Cludgy and Arthur started pleasantly enough. The chickens had provided some eggs

207

for breakfast. They went to church and sang all the favourite carols. Afterwards Reverend Peterson stopped them as they left the church.

'I had a phone call this morning just before I left.' He turned to Lindy.

'Lindy, your father is coming over to see you, and should arrive sometime tomorrow morning.' Her face lit up! She was so happy, she ran and told Reggie and Auntie Bee and then everyone else in the congregation whether they wanted to know or not!

Lindy danced all the way back to the cottage: she hopped and skipped with her arms in the air.

'Anyone would think,' said Arthur solemnly, 'that she had had some good news.'

'Don't tease her,' said Cludgy. 'This is wonderful news. She deserves it. She has had to get over losing her mother like that and then be separated from her dad.'

At home Arthur lit the sitting room fire, and they sat and gave each other their presents. Cludgy gave Arthur a new woolly hat in navy blue, she also gave one to Lindy, but hers had lots of different colours.

'It's like a rainbow,' Lindy said.

Arthur gave Cludgy a carved model of a fish. He had whittled it out of a piece of driftwood found on the beach.

Lindy gave Arthur a silly story about Goat learning how to fish. Arthur stood up and read this in a funny voice with actions to match which made his female audience laugh. Lindy gave Cludgy a painted stone, similar to that

208

made by Reggie for his mother. Her stone was much bigger.

'I'll keep that on the windowsill by the sink: it will look nice there.'

There was one parcel left to open. 'It's from your dad. Do you want to open it now or wait for tomorrow and he can give it to you himself?'

Lindy took it in her hands and held it close to her.

'It would be nice for him to see me open it,' she said, 'but if I open it now, I'll have a whole day of enjoying it before he comes.' She paused. 'I'll open it now!'

'Save the string and paper!' said Cludgy. 'You never know when it will be useful.'

The parcel was wrapped in brown paper and tied up with hairy string. Lindy looked for the knot. With nimble fingers and patience, she carefully undid it. William had rolled the item in the paper, and once free of the string the gift tumbled out onto the floor. In front of Lindy lay an oblong box. She carefully opened it. First, she found a note from her father. 'This is for you to write your lovely letters to me,' it said.

'It's a fountain pen!' said Cludgy.

'It's Mummy's pen!' Lindy said, and tears rushed to her eyes.

Cludgy held her as she sobbed on her shoulder. 'There, there precious, you just cry all you like.'

'But I must be strong! Mummy said,' she sobbed, 'if I cry, I'm not strong.'

Just for a moment Cludgy did not know what to say. She held her until the tears subsided.

'Crying does not show weakness: running away from problems and difficulties does. You're strong and you've been very brave this last year. We're very proud of you and so would your mother be. Pick up the pen and let's have a look at it.' Lindy took her handkerchief from her pocket, wiped her eyes and blew her nose.

The pen was green, with a band around the lid that was gold, as was the clip for holding it in a pocket or on a tie. She unscrewed the top and revealed the nib that was also gold. As she held it as if to write, she could see her mother using it.

Arthur disappeared from the room and came back with a bottle of ink, blotting paper and a piece of white card. 'There, now let's fill the pen, and you can start writing with it.'

Using the lever Lindy carefully filled the pen, wiped it on some blotting paper and then started to write.

She wrote: 'Happy Christmas!'

Lunch had to be accredited to some clever bartering by Arthur. He had done some digging for a farmer for nothing, and he had grown a glut of potatoes, carrots and greens and swapped the work and the vegetables for a joint of pork! When Cludgy saw the joint, she picked it up and announced, 'that will last us for three days at least!'

Wearing their new woolly hats, Arthur and Lindy sat down as Cludgy served up a lovely roast dinner. Ever frugal, Cludgy had carved the meat to make sure there was enough for dinner tomorrow when William came.

Only Cludgy knew what was in the Christmas pudding, but there was a lucky silver threepenny piece that Lindy found.

'The pudding was different,' said Arthur, 'but nice enough. Don't you agree Lindy?'

'Oh yes, nice enough,' she repeated.

Reggie, Auntie Bee and Robert came round in the afternoon, which was spent in the sitting room by the fire playing parlour games. Lindy kept score where it was needed using her new pen. They sang the carol game: where each team had to sing a different Christmas carol that had not been sung before in the game. Arthur, Robert and Reggie worked as a team, but were outclassed by Betsy, Cludgy and Lindy as they went on for quite a while as they knew far more.

28
Daddy

The blackout was still up when Lindy opened her eyes on Boxing Day. She went to the window and took the blackouts down and saw that it was morning. 'Daddy!' she said to herself, as she laid back and stretched on her bed. 'Daddy is coming today!'

It was no good, she could not stay in bed any longer. Usually, Cludgy called her for breakfast when it was time to get up. 'Breakfast will be ready in five minutes,' she would call. 'Up you get! You mustn't be late for school.' Or she might say, 'The sun is shining, the birds are up! They're singing and waiting for you to get up!'

Today she had heard nothing. She lay there pondering. *Do I get up now? It may be too early. Do I wait for Cludgy to call? My daddy is coming today so I'll get up*, she decided. *He may come early*.

She dressed and clambered downstairs. Arthur was in the kitchen. 'Shush, Cludgy is still asleep! Would you help me see to the chickens? They may have laid some eggs for our breakfast!'

Lindy turned back to the stairs, ready to apologise to Cludgy for making a noise, then stopped herself as she would have to make a noise to call out 'Sorry'.

She picked up the basket, Arthur took a bowl of chicken feed and they walked across the lane through the vegetable garden to the henhouse. Lindy found four eggs

212

and placed them carefully in the basket. 'One each, and one for Mr A. N. Otherday,' quipped Arthur. Lindy laughed, although she had heard that joke many times before.

'What's the time Arthur please?'

'It's around eight o'clock. And before you ask, the boats from Portsmouth go every hour and a half. Well it takes the boat one hour, that's 60 minutes to cross the Solent. That is if all goes well. If the weather is inclement and the sea is rough, it can take an hour and a half - that's 90 minutes! They could of course have a good crossing and arrive early.'

'Arthur!' said Lindy exasperated. 'Please, what time do the boats get in?'

'Oh, you want to know when the boats get in from Portsmouth at Ryde Pier. The eight o'clock from Portsmouth gets in at nine o'clock, and then the next one is around about ten o'clock or half past ten.

'So, he could be at Ryde pier at nine o'clock,' deduced Lindy.

'Or thereabouts, maybe nine o'clock, ... or half past nine, ... or ten.'

They all had eggs for breakfast. Mr Otherday's egg was stored safely away in the cool larder. Lindy ate her boiled egg and toast as fast as she could.

'Mind you don't get indigestion!' Cludgy warned.

'You always say that, and I never do!'

'Lindy, you can leave the washing up to me today.

213

You go and wait for your dad. Arthur will help instead.'

'Arthur! will do what?' said Arthur.

In her winter coat and new rainbow woolly hat, Lindy stood outside the cottage. She looked to her right. *He could come on the bus and walk down the lane,* she pondered, *or he could come along Ladies Lane.* Just as she thought that, she saw a navy-blue peaked cap bobbing up and down as if it was walking up the hill. As the hat got nearer, it got higher and she saw a face, then shoulders, and soon a whole body. It was her daddy! She ran to him, 'Daddy, Daddy!' she shouted. He scooped her up and held her tight. Lindy's arms were firmly around his shoulders, her face pressed against his cheek.

They stopped hugging, leaned back and looked at each other. Then they hugged each other again.

'I'm so glad to see you!' they said together.

William put his daughter down, and hand in hand they walked the last few yards to the cottage. Arthur and Cludgy were outside, as they had heard Lindy's shout that had announced his arrival.

'How do you do?' said Cludgy. 'This is my husband, Arthur.' They all shook hands, greeting each other warmly. 'Would you like to have a cup of tea?' offered Cludgy.

'That would be wonderful! it was quite a walk from the pier to Little Bridge!' William said.

'I bet you haven't had any breakfast!' Cludgy remarked.

'Well, you're right there. I got the earliest boat I could. I was on duty last night.'

'No raid?' asked Arthur.

'No, thank goodness, no raid.'

'Lindy! Would you please get Mr Otherday's egg from the larder? Would you like it boiled William?'

'A real egg! Yes please! But I don't want to take an egg out of another man's mouth. Will Mr Otherday mind me stealing his egg?'

William could not understand why they were all laughing. Cludgy explained the joke.

Lindy sat close to her dad as he tucked into the boiled egg, two pieces of toast and a large cup of tea.

'Now I suggest,' Cludgy began, 'that you two go out together. Lindy is looking forward to showing you where she lives, and then come back here for lunch. I've some left-over pork from yesterday.'

'A real egg for breakfast, and pork for dinner! I'm being treated like a king.'

Putting on her coat and warm hat again, Lindy said, 'I'll show you the church where the incendiaries fell, and then the beach.'

Lindy held her father's hand tightly as they walked up to the church. Standing hand in hand looking at the door and the front of the church, she showed him where Reggie's father had climbed up the outside of the building.

They then went down the hill to the beach, and she recounted the story of the German pilot. They sat on the

215

beach cuddled together, 'And this is where I sit and look over to Portsmouth and think of you.'

'And over there,' said William, pointing to Portsmouth, 'is where your pin-man double waves to my pin-man double.'

Lindy laughed. She felt so happy.

As they walked back to the cottage for lunch, Lindy let slip 'That's the golf course where Reggie stole the golf balls.' She gasped and quickly covered her mouth.

'He what?' said her father. 'He stole golf balls?'

'Yes, but I made him give them all back!'

Lindy recounted the story. Before she had finished, they were laughing so much their sides ached.

'I would have loved to have seen that policeman's face when he found his saddle bag half filled with golf-balls.' William was crying with laughter now. He wiped his face.

'But you mustn't tell Cludgy,' instructed Lindy, 'or Arthur or Auntie Bee, as they don't know anything about it at all.'

William crossed his fingers. 'I promise, it's our secret.'

As they walked back to the cottage every now and then they laughed as they remembered the golf balls and the policeman. They had a lovely lunch of cold pork with apple sauce, mashed potatoes, steamed carrots and a delicious sauce made from bottled tomatoes.

'It's a funny combination, I'm afraid,' Cludgy said in

an apologetic tone.

'All the more delicious,' William replied.

'Apple fritters for pudding?' Cludgy asked.

'It has all been delicious, thank you so much. Thank you also for looking after my Lindy. She is so happy here.'

The weather had turned and Cludgy offered to light the fire in the sitting room for them to sit and perhaps play some board games. The fire had been laid, as Cludgy had anticipated they would need to stay in. She lit the paper, and it took immediately. 'You know how to lay a fire,' said William.

'Years of training!' replied Cludgy.

William did not quite understand. The card table was set up and there were some games left from the day before.

'There you are, I'll leave you to it.' Cludgy left the room.

The green pen lay on the card table. Lindy picked it up and looked at her dad. 'I love the pen. It writes really well.'

'It's a beautiful pen,' said William. 'You deserve to have it, your mother would be so proud of you. Of that, I am sure.'

They played Ludo, which was Lindy's favourite, and a game called 'Old Maid' with the pack of cards. They were so happy in each other's company that the afternoon flew by. Cludgy came in. 'I must put up the blackout curtains now,' she said.

217

'Let me help you!' said William as he passed her the large square frames with blackout curtain material nailed on in the middle of them. They fitted snugly into each window.

'You can turn the light on now, Lindy, please,' said Cludgy.

Lindy was now suddenly aware that it was time for her father to go back to Portsmouth.

'You'll have some tea and cake before you leave?' Cludgy offered.

'Oh, you must have a piece of Cludgy's cake,' Lindy said, 'She's a genius at cake making!' There was a tight knot in her stomach: she did not want to let her daddy go now. She knew she had to be brave again.

Cuddling her dad, she said, 'I'm sick of being brave.'

'But you do it very well,' said her father. 'I've something to tell you. In the raid just before Christmas our house was bombed. I'm afraid there's nothing left of it. I've been living at the station since then. Being over here with you now gave me the idea that perhaps I can transfer to a fire station on the island, and we can be closer to each other.'

'That would be wonderful!' Lindy smiled.

They ate their cake and drank their tea.

'It was a delicious cake. Thank you Cludgy,' said William, then he looked at Lindy. 'I don't want to take you back to Portsmouth: it's not a nice place at the moment. I've left my new address with Cludgy. Geoff, my section commander, said that my letters could be accepted there until I can find some digs. There is one good thing though ...'

'What's that?' asked Lindy

'There's nowhere for Aunt Joan to come and stay.'

'Daddy, that's not very nice!'

They laughed together.

Arthur suggested that William get a bus back to Ryde. I'll walk with you both to the bus stop at the bottom of Little Bridge hill. Then, Lindy, we can walk back together,' said Arthur. 'It's too dark for you to walk alone.'

Parting was horrid! Lindy and William waved and waved as they had done when Lindy was on the Isle of Wight ferry last May. Then she did not stop until her father was out of sight. Again, they continued to wave until they couldn't see each other anymore. It was a good thing that it was so dark that night, as Lindy cried silently all the way back to the cottage. She turned the doorknob and Cludgy called out, 'Alright pet?'

Lindy sniffed; 'Yes, I'm alright, thanks,' she replied. *There's that word again*, she thought.

29
Discovering New Talents

Lindy and Reggie saw little of each other after Christmas. The weather had taken a turn for the worse and it was becoming quite cold to play out. For Christmas Auntie Bee had given Reggie her small box of paints, which had further stimulated the artistic streak in him. Obviously in collusion with Auntie Bee, his mother, Shirley, had sent him a large pad of white paper, pencils, a rubber and a pencil sharpener. He tried to keep the pad for 'best', and use only odd scraps of paper that Auntie Bee and Cludgy could find. He used backs of envelopes, cereal packets and brown wrapping paper that had been ironed smooth.

Deep in his shed and hidden for years, Arthur had found an old frame with a wooden back that he gave to Reggie. There was no glass front or picture in it. 'Perhaps you could frame one of your pictures?' suggested Arthur.

'Thanks,' said Reggie, 'but I think I've a better idea than just a picture.'

'Come with me, Lindy,' he said, 'I want to go to the beach and collect shells and stick them on the wooden back in an abstract pattern.' Since he had created the paperweight for his mum with a pattern made of dots, he had learnt the meaning of the word abstract.

They put on their warmest clothes, their hats and mittens, before venturing out to go the short distance down the hill to the beach. It was a bitterly cold day, more especially on the beach. 'Can you find me lots of little shells, it's only a small frame?' requested Reggie.

They stuffed their pockets with limpets, periwinkles and yellow cowrie shells. They searched among the big rocks for the smallest and most brightly coloured stones. Lindy was fascinated by the slipper limpets as they looked like a baby's cradle. 'I'm going to call these cradle shells,' she announced.

Lindy ran her hands through the soft sand and thought about the warm summer when they had played on the beach. *The sand looks no different than it did in August. Then it was inviting, as we walked on it. But touching it now is uncomfortably cold.*

They didn't waste time getting back to the cottages. The cold seemed to creep in under their coats and hats. 'My nose is freezing!' announced Reggie. 'Do you think it'd fall off if I knocked it?'

'Do you want me to try?' asked Lindy.

'No, you leave my nose alone!'

'You can be sure that it won't fall off!'

They both went into Auntie Bee's cottage first, where they emptied out their pockets onto the dining room table.

'This is my studio here,' said Reggie, who couldn't wait to get started on his abstract design. 'Lindy, could you go and ask Cludgy if I can borrow the glue pot?'

'Please,' said Auntie Bee, 'say please.'

'Please, Lindy.'

221

'Oh Reggie, you do do things back to front! How did you expect to stick the shells on without glue? AND how do you know that she will let you have the glue? Surely you should've checked if you had all you needed before you started?'

'Cludgy's lovely. I'm sure she will,' Reggie said sweetly.

Lindy stomped home. She was furious.

'Reggie has such a cheek!' she yelled at Cludgy. 'He's asked me to come and get the glue pot so he can stick his bloomin' shells in his frame. We went to the beach and collected the shells, and he had no way of sticking them! He expects to get the glue without asking first! What a cheek!'

'Oh,' said Cludgy softly.

'Then he has asked me to ask you if he can **borrow** it! I ask you, **borrow it**?' Lindy was screeching now. 'Borrowing means that you give it back. How can he give it back if he's used it to stick his shells in the frame?'

'I know, I know,' Cludgy said sweetly. 'Of course, I'll let him have some. Would you take it around to him please?'

'Then he expects me to deliver it for him. Humph! Cheek, what cheek!'

'It keeps him out of trouble,' said Cludgy as she looked sympathetically at her and smiled. Lindy relented.

'Alright I'll do it for **you**, not **Reggie**!' She stomped out of the kitchen door, shutting it noisily behind her and walked the few steps next door. In the meantime, Auntie Bee had had 'words' with Reggie, who in turn thanked Lindy for her trouble and asked that she in turn would thank Cludgy. There was nothing for Lindy to do at Auntie Bee's, other than watch Reggie sort his shells for his abstract masterpiece he was creating. She turned toward the door. 'See you later!' she called out.

'Bye!' said Auntie Bee. 'Reggie! Lindy is going, what should you say to your friend?'

'Oh yeah, bye!' was all he could manage as he was so engrossed in sorting out the different beach stones from the shells.

Lindy found Cludgy by her fire in the sitting room, the radio was on, and she was holding a jam jar. In it was some creamy white liquid. The lid was fixed tightly.

'I'm going to make some butter! Would you like to help me please?' she asked. Lindy was perplexed. 'I'll show you. Butter is made from cream. They have big butter churns at the dairy that have handles that are turned by hand. This can take quite a while and it's tiring work. We're going to make a small amount in a jam-jar. I've saved the top of the milk from three pints, which is put in the jar with a little salt. Now we have to shake the jar like this. For a long, long … time! So, we take it in turns. Eventually we should end up with a lump of butter and some watery liquid called whey.' The shaking action was shared between the two of them as they listened to the radio. 'It's quite a tiring job,' commented Lindy.

223

'I know, but the butter we'll get is lovely. I'll make sure we, the workers, get our fair share.'

'And Arthur, doesn't he deserve any?'

'Well, I suppose so, I'll give him a little.' They giggled!

Lindy was not sure how long the two of them sat shaking the jam jar, but eventually in the jar was a lump of golden butter. It was during her turn to shake when Cludgy shouted out, 'It's turned! Look Lindy, we've made butter!'

The next morning with their toast, Cludgy had shared out the precious butter between the three of them. Cludgy and Lindy spread their allotted amount on their toast and then they ate it slowly. 'I want to savour every mouthful!' said Lindy.

Lindy was anxious to see Arthur's reaction to all their hard work. Cludgy had spread his share of the butter already on his toast. Lindy and Cludgy watched him closely as he sat down, picked up his toast and almost in one mouthful scoffed it down.

'Arthur! If you only knew the trouble and time it took to make that butter you would have given it more respect!' said Cludgy.

'We churned that in a jam-jar **ALL** afternoon yesterday,' added Lindy, 'and it took you two seconds to eat it!'

'No, three seconds at least!' said Arthur.

Lindy and Cludgy, who still had some of their toast and homemade butter to eat, scowled at him!

224

30
Imagination

School over, Reggie and Lindy walked home together. They quickened their steps as it was bitterly cold. When they reached the cottages, the sky was so clear that the stars appeared like diamonds, shiny and sparkling. Cludgy was in the kitchen getting supper ready. She had prepared her basket and bag for a night in the shelter.

'I've put an extra blanket there for you. Whether Hitler comes or not, it's going to be very cold tonight.'

They had not long finished their supper, when the siren howled out its usual nightly warning.

'Here we go Lindy, pick up your stuff and let's get in the shelter.' Cludgy filled up the Thermos and picked up the basket and some of the blankets. Lindy, now dressed in her coat and woolly hat and mittens, took the rest of the blankets and two pillows. It was just past 6 o'clock when they walked to their shelter. Betsy and Reggie next door were already in theirs. 'Goodnight Cludgy, goodnight Lindy!' she called out.

'Goodnight!' Cludgy and Lindy replied.

'Good for who?' Cludgy muttered, 'Hitler or us?'

In the shelter, Lindy got into her bunk. Cludgy sat down on the wooden chair by the candle and started knitting.

'What are you knitting?' asked Lindy.

'A school jumper,' said Cludgy.

225

'Who is it for?'

'Alan Rodgers, he's five. His mother has problems with her hands. So, I said I would do it.'

'What problems?'

'I don't know, but she can't knit.'

226

Lindy lay in her bunk, it was very quiet. All she could hear was the clicking of knitting needles.

'It's so silent! There is no noise at all.' said Lindy after a while. 'Maybe they've got it wrong and there's to be no raid, the all-clear siren will go off and we can go back into the house and sleep in our lovely warm beds.'

'I wish!' replied Cludgy. 'I tell you what we can do: we'll play a game. You've got to shut your eyes tight and imagine that you are snuggled up in your bed. Your head is on the white pillow case, the cotton sheets are newly washed and ironed. The blankets are soft and light. Can you feel them Lindy?'

'Yes, if I think really hard. Don't forget my bright red quilt.'

'Oh yes, imagine you are touching it, it's smooth and silky.'

'What are you going to imagine for yourself? Where are you in your imagination?'

'Oh, that's easy, I'm by the fireside in the sitting room knitting. I'm resting my feet on the stool and warming them by the fire.'

She continued with her imaginary game, but Lindy was fast asleep. She awoke at seven, as a wave of bombers droned noisily overhead.

'Bother!' Cludgy said.

'They weren't wrong. Here they come!' Lindy said.

Almost immediately there were sharp staccato sounds of the anti-aircraft guns being fired. They were so

227

used to air-raids that any fear they had felt at the beginning of these raids had disappeared. Lindy put her head back on her pillow, pulled the blanket up to her neck in an attempt to drop off to sleep again.

She went back to the imaginary game, but this time she imagined it was summer and she was walking with her daddy along the beach. She imagined his hand holding hers, she imagined looking up at him, she saw his bronzed arms from the sunshine. In her mind she heard the waves rushing in and slipping back, and saw her feet in the cool water as she paddled.

Arthur came home at eight o'clock. 'Hello,' he said, 'I've come to bring Texi home, he doesn't want to walk with me tonight. It's very noisy, I suppose.'

Cludgy lifted Texi up to his new place on Lindy's bunk and settled. His basket had long been expelled from the shelter as being too bulky and taking up too much room. He settled quickly, making his three circles before flopping down at the end of the bed. He had had quite enough of patrolling around with his master in all that noise.

'Cup of tea before you go back?' said Cludgy.

'No thanks, best get going!' Cludgy joined him outside the door of the shelter. He lowered his voice down to a whisper. 'It looks like Portsmouth is getting it tonight. There are a lot of fires over there.'

At the word of Portsmouth Lindy's eyes opened. She lifted her head from the pillow.

'Yes,' Arthur continued, 'it's a very clear night, the

228

stars are sparkling, but my goodness, nothing can compare with the intense and angry glow over Portsmouth. The sky is red. They're very busy over there tonight for sure.'

Lindy lay still. She suddenly had a strong need to see her daddy. Her imagination suddenly turned to him in his fireman's uniform. *I want to see him now!* she said to herself. *If I can't see him, I can see Portsmouth, where he is.* In a silly way she was sure that if she could see Portsmouth, she could imagine him more clearly.

At the door of the shelter, Cludgy said goodbye to Arthur.

'Be careful, make sure you're safe, won't you,' he said as he kissed her.

'Of course I will, I'm not stupid,' she replied, 'I'm going to make a cup of tea with the hot water I have in the Thermos.'

Cludgy climbed back into the shelter and reached for her thermos flask. She shook it. It was empty. She checked on Lindy who was lying still in the bunk. Assuming she was asleep she slipped out, entered the house through the kitchen door and put the kettle on.

Lindy spotted her chance. She was going to go down to the beach and see Portsmouth. Carefully she stuffed one of the pillows under the blankets to make it look like she was in bed. Patting Texi on the head she jumped down to the cobbled floor, pulled out her wellington boots from under the bottom bunk, put them on and

229

poked her head out of the door. She looked left and right first, before she went through the door and ran to the lane.

It was such a clear night the route was plainly visible all the way to the beach. She ran down the path to the shore and, despite the continuous drone of the German aeroplanes, she heard the waves, and then turned the corner onto the sand. She looked over to Portsmouth where there was this massive red sky hanging over the city. At first, she was speechless! It was such a terrifying sight. She remembered daddy saying, 'Red sky at night, shepherds' delight.' This wasn't a friendly red sky, where shepherds were happy, this was evil. Underneath this red glow, she knew her daddy was working.

'Daddy, DADDY!' she cried out. 'Why are you still working over there? You should be with me!' She riled at her mother for dying, at Hitler, at the fire brigade for having him work there, at God and everyone who had made her feel this way. She screamed and shouted for a while until, exhausted, she then dropped down on the sand and sobbed.

Back in the shelter, Cludgy finished her tea, and Texi got up and moved his place further up the bunk. He sat on the lump caused by the pillow that Lindy had placed.

'Texi, come here, you naughty boy,' said Cludgy. 'You'll wake Lindy up.'

She lifted the dog from the bunk and the lump stayed flat. She tore back the blankets and realised that Lindy wasn't there.

'Oh, my goodness,' she screamed, 'Lindy's gone!'

Betsy came out of her shelter and called out, 'What's up, Cludgy?'

'Lindy's disappeared! I was only in the house a short while, just to fill my flask up again.'

'Right, keep calm.' said Betsy. 'In that short time, she can't have gone far. Let's try and work out why, and then we might discover where she's gone.'

'She was fine when we came to the shelter at six. She was her usual helpful self. Arthur came home to let Texi have a rest. Oh, my goodness, she must have been awake when Arthur told me that Portsmouth was in flames.'

'But where would she go having heard that news?'

'She'll be on the beach,' said a voice from behind. As soon as he had heard Cludgy shout, Reggie got up. 'When we're down there, she often talks about her dad. She says it's the place that she feels closest to him. I'll go and get her if you like.'

'No, no, thanks all the same Reggie, I'll go,' said Cludgy, 'and take Texi with me.'

'And I'll make some fresh hot water bottles to warm up her bed, said Betsy. 'She's going to be cold.'

'But that means you'll be in your kitchen, you need to be in the shelter. It's not safe in our houses,' warned Cludgy.

'Oh, don't worry about me,' replied Betsy, 'the Jerries are too busy bombing Portsmouth to worry about

Little Bridge.

Taking a blanket with her, Cludgy set off down the hill to the beach. Texi ran on in front.

'That's right, go and find Lindy! Off you go!' Texi shot off like a bullet from a gun, straight down the hill, turned left at the bridge and continued at speed along the path to the beach.

'I thought Arthur brought you home because you were tired! Texi - you're a little liar.'

Cludgy got to the bridge and started calling for Lindy, hoping that perhaps she might come down the path to meet her.

'Lindy, come home!' she shouted. She strained her eyes towards the end of the path and was greeted by a violent red sky. She realised that Lindy was witnessing the horror of what was happening across the water in Portsmouth.

Seated on the cold sand, with her head on her knees, Lindy suddenly felt the warm breath and body of Texi before she realised it was him. How lovely it was to feel this furry warm creature against her. She stroked his soft head and cuddled him. 'We must go home,' she said to the dog. 'I shouldn't have come.'

She stood up ready to walk back, and Texi barked and barked. Cludgy heard him, and hoped that he had found her. Cludgy shouted. 'Lindy, Lindy, where are you?'

'I'm here, I'm here!' she yelled back.

'There you are! What were you thinking?' snapped

Cludgy. She was relieved, but she was very angry. How could a sensible girl like Lindy be so stupid as to go to the beach in the middle of the night during an air raid warning and in freezing cold January.

'I'm sorry, I'm so sorry!' Lindy started to cry again as Cludgy wrapped a warm blanket around her.

'Alright, alright, we'll talk about it in the morning.'

31
Meanwhile

As Lindy went to the shelter that night her dad, William, rode his bike to work. It was a clear night. He often thought of what was in store for him at work that day. There had been raids in the late summer, autumn and winter, and the public were changing their minds that these newly enrolled men were fifty bob a week army dodgers. Even the regular firemen, who had been doing the job for years, had more respect for these volunteers. There had been no raids since the 23rd of December, 1940. He had managed to get over to the island and see Lindy on Boxing Day, but the fear of more raids meant that his visit was short. Firemen were needed in Portsmouth.

He arrived at the station a little late for parade. He parked his bike. There was a full complement there that day, the 10th of January, 1941. Section commander Geoff Knight stood bold upright and stared directly at William, who spluttered, 'Sorry I'm a little late, I had to post a letter to Lindy.'

The eight men stood to attention. Their fireman's axes, their only piece of personal equipment, were checked that all were intact and not missing. Some of the lads had torches, but they weren't official issue. William had a small torch, but the battery was failing and getting a replacement was very difficult. There were none available, as everyone wanted them.

'How's the Rolls today, Ronald? Fit and ready for duty I hope.' Ronald Demby-Smythe owned an ancient Rolls Royce, and it was used to tow the pump needed to get water from the supplementary water supply tanks, which were placed throughout the city, to the fire.

'Oh yes sir,' he replied. 'Topping sir, filled with fuel and ready for action!'

'I see all of you have taken my advice,' the section commander continued rather pompously, 'and added pieces of leather onto the backs of your helmets. That should prevent hot embers and other debris from going down the backs of your necks and inside your tunics.'

Fred Kedderidge, another member of the team, whispered, 'I'm not sure it was his idea, I've seen them used elsewhere'.

'Well done, chaps!' Geoff announced.

At 7 o'clock the phone rang, and shortly afterwards all the lights went out.

'Have they forgotten to pay the electricity bill?' said Charlie Rudd.

'Anyone got a coin for the meter?' quipped Rod Haynes.

Explosions were heard in the distance. 'They must have got the power station,' William said.

Geoff went to answer the phone, just as bombs and incendiaries started to fall on Portsmouth. The watch went to their vehicles. 'We've been told to report to the Guildhall!' he shouted.

235

They set off.   There were seven men in the fire tender. Fred Kedderidge was driving, and Geoff was in the front seat.   Clinging on to the back were the other members of the team: William, Charley King, Rod Haynes and Harry Hinks.   And in his own vehicle behind was Ronald Demby-Smythe. His Rolls Royce was rather old and had been fitted with a tow bar to tow the pump. It had been looked after well and had not been used much. Ronald described it 'as reliable and as solid as a tank'. It was ideal for the job for which it was being used.

'Although it does use of lot of petrol,' said Ronald, when he offered its services for the job of towing the pump.

'Needs must,' said Geoff, 'needs must.'

Ronald was rather pleased originally, as he was about to get some free fuel. Petrol coupons were very difficult to get hold off. When not being used for the fire service, he could drive his Rolls anywhere.

With the trailer jogging along behind as if a servant to a great lord and master, the Rolls Royce made its way through the streets of Portsmouth, already littered with bricks and debris. It was a massive raid. The pump was very much needed that night. In every street there was a fire in at least one of the buildings. They turned down Palmerston Road and were faced with walls of fire on both sides. There wasn't a single shop or house not burning. Handley's, the large store on the corner which sold practically everything, was a mass of flames that poured out of every window.

As they approached the Guildhall the extent of the damage to the building was visible. The whole of the roof from back to front was alight.

'The roof,' said Charley, 'is constructed totally out of wood. That's why the fire must have caught hold so quickly.'

'What an awful sight,' said William, 'it was such a magnificent construction.'

Section commander Geoff pondered as to what they could do to be of any use in fighting such a large fire. He jumped down and walked towards the divisional commander who was walking towards him.

'There's nothing you lads can do here,' he said sadly. 'There's no water! The mains have been bombed. The Guildhall is going to have to be left to burn.'

'What do you want us to do then?' asked Geoff.

'There are, as you know, lots of emergency water tanks around the city. Go and find anyone of those which is near a burning building and do what you can.'

The tender obediently left the sad scene. The proud Portsmouth Guildhall was burning, and they could do nothing to help. Even if they had mains water, how would they have been of any use putting out such an enormous fire?

'I know it's awful, lads,' said Geoff, 'but it's only a building.'

'Only a building! That's the Guildhall!' someone

muttered from behind him.

'No one has been hurt, no one was killed, they got out in time,' Geoff said. 'Our job is to save lives first and put out fires. Now let's concentrate on finding a water tank and a fire we can help with. Does anyone know this area, where we can find one of those supplementary water supply tanks?'

'Why not try King Edward Grove?' Charley said. 'There are lots of terraced houses there. I'm sure there must be a tank.'

'Right' said Geoff, 'look out for the SWS signs!'

As they drove through the city looking for a suitable combination of water tank and burning building, bombs were falling all around, and incendiaries were dropping like rain. It was hard for the younger firemen to hide their fear. It wasn't long before they found the right combination. There was a small 50,000-gallon tank full of water and a fire in the upper rooms of a terraced house down the street. Between them and the house was a lot of rubble and bricks scattered around from another explosion. There was an empty space where a house had been.

'Must have had a direct hit,' said young Harry.

As soon as the fire engine arrived a lady with an ARP hat on ran up towards them. 'Don't worry about number four,' she said, pointing to the destroyed house. 'They weren't in. They'd already gone to the shelter.'

'Right,' said Geoff, pointing to a house with flames

coming from the roof and upstairs bedroom windows. 'What about that one?'.

'There's an old lady in that house. I've not seen her come out,' a neighbour shouted.

'What's her name?' asked Geoff.

'We call her Dotty,' said another neighbour, ''cos she is!'

'Does she answer to the name of Dotty?' enquired Geoff in a serious voice.

'NO, NO, DON'T CALL HER THAT! She thinks she's much better than us. She's Mrs Dorothy Withers,' said the neighbour. 'She insists on being called Mrs Withers.'

Just then Ronald called out 'Sorry Geoff, I'm not going to be able to get the Rolls any further. There's too much rubble.'

'Yes, I know,' he replied. 'We're going to have trouble getting the tender closer too. Charley! Can you help move some of the rubble!' The tender and the Rolls Royce with its trailer gingerly edged forward as far as they could.

'That's far enough!' shouted Geoff. 'The water tank's just over there. Let's move the trailer by hand now.'

The firemen knew what to do. They unhitched the pump and manoeuvred the heavy trailer through the bricks and chunks of concrete that littered the road to a place nearer the water tank. Ronald left his car and helped Charley shift some of the debris.

The men worked in pairs: one was starting the engine of the pump, the others were preparing the hoses ready to use on the fire.

'William and Charley, will you go in and look for her? I hope she's downstairs, there's not a lot left of upstairs!'

'Oh yes, she'll be on the ground floor,' shouted the neighbour. 'She lives and sleeps downstairs and doesn't use the upper floor. She says it's to save money.'

Aware of falling debris or hot ash from above, the two men adjusted their helmets and their improvised flaps for protection from hot embers.

With their torches lit, William ventured in with Charley behind. Crawling on the floor they approached with caution, looking around for Mrs Withers and to avoid any dangers.

'The upper floor's holding at the moment!' shouted Charley.

'Mrs Withers, are you there?' William called out. 'It's the fire brigade. We're here to help you.'

'Hello,' came a reply from the kitchen. 'I'm just getting a bucket of water; I've got my stirrup pump here. I've got an incendiary upstairs. I think it's gone off!'

'It has, my dear,' said William. 'We're here to lead you out. I'm afraid your upper floor's well alight.'

With all the noise and shouting, the firemen hadn't heard the faint sound of a dog barking.

'I'm not going without my little Pickle,' said Mrs Withers.

'Pickle! Who's Pickle?' asked William.

'He's my dog. Can't you hear him? He's in the back

room, I shut him in there so he wouldn't get in the way when I was putting out the incendiary.'

'Now Mrs Withers, Charley will lead you out first, and I'll go to the back room and get err ... little Pickle.

'Yes, my little Pickle! And he's such a naughty scamp. But I love him.'

Mrs Withers was very calm and seemed oblivious of the danger she was in as Charlie led her out. Except for a small amount of smoke just visible downstairs, it wasn't apparent from their position in her hall that the top of her house was alight. The fireman held their hoses tight ready to play the water on the flames coming from the upstairs windows.

As she reached the edge of the pavement outside her house, she turned around. 'Oh my Gawd, me 'ouse is on fire!' she yelled.

'Yes, we know, that's why we're here,' said Charley in the calmest of tones that he could muster. 'William has gone to the backroom to get little Pickle for you.'

'WATER ON!' shouted the fireman at the front of the hose, as he raised his fist in the air.

The pump operator, Ronald, raised his fist in reply and shouted, 'WATER ON!' as he simultaneously wound open the delivery valve. The water rushed out of the hose and into the upstairs bedroom window of Mrs Withers' house.

Back downstairs William ventured along the corridor to the back room. The door was closed. Expecting to find

241

a nervous little dog William, already crouched down, called sweetly, 'Pickle! Pickle! There's a good little Pickle.'

He reached up to the door handle, turned it and opened it carefully. The blackout curtains had been put up, there was no light anywhere in the room. William was greeted by an unseen low menacing growl. He turned on his small torch, which shone weakly into the room. The feeble beam came to rest on two wide open eyes. It was Pickle. He was obviously on guard protecting his home. His deep growl was now accompanied by a vicious bark that was meant to put fear into his opponent. It did.

William cleared his throat, and in the sweetest voice he could muster called out, 'Come on Pickle! There's a good boy!'

William was still crouching in the middle of the door frame. He was, according to Pickle, an intruder and in the line of fire. The large stout bulldog shot towards him at such a speed that William had no chance. The dog pounced, hitting William's shoulder and pushing him to the ground. He was now flat on his back; his helmet lay beside him. Pickle, now free from his dark imprisonment, bounded over him and made for the open front door. However, as William was trying to recover himself from the floor of the hall, at that exact moment there was an explosion and then a rumbling sound. The floor and the whole house shook, showering William with lathe and plaster from the ceiling above. William covered his face with his arm. There was so much debris on him, he was going to need help to get out. Before he could shout, there was a further rumble and more of the ceiling and upper floor fell, hitting him on the head.

32
Nothing

Lindy spent the rest of the night back in the shelter, sleeping with Texi one side of her and a hot water bottle the other. No harm had come to her. The next morning, she sat down at the kitchen table to write a letter to her father. But she was at a loss as to what to write. She couldn't tell him about how she ran down to the beach in the middle of the night. She knew she had been wrong to do so, even before Cludgy had sat her down and spoke seriously about how dangerous her actions had been.

She hadn't been back at school for long, so there was not a lot to tell him about that. In any case the days were so disrupted with late starts owing to the air raids. All she had to write about school was that she was doing very well and enjoyed it. Miss Simons had given her lots of extra work to do. She loved the essays, but found the arithmetic difficult to do. Miss Simons constantly assured her, that it was just logic and it would get easier the more she practised.

She wrote about Reggie's new artistic talent but didn't want to tell him that they had a row over his shell collage. Lindy felt that he was using her like a servant running errands for him to collect the glue while he sat creating his masterpiece.

Lindy wanted to write nice things and her argument with Reggie wasn't: it was horrid.

She was stuck with nothing. Nothing to tell him at all. She asked Cludgy. She sighed! 'Now what can you tell him? We sang your favourite Epiphany hymn in church on Sunday last.'

Lindy wrote about that in one sentence!

'I tell you what we should do,' said Cludgy. 'Put down the letter and finish it later. I've got some shopping to do in Ryde. We'll do that and then maybe that will inspire you with something to tell him.'

Armed with their ration books, they went on the bus into Ryde, then walked up the town to their allotted grocer. There was a small queue there. They couldn't see the customer at the front of the queue, as she was sitting down. Lindy moved to the side to get a better view. She was a large lady with a rather faded felt hat. A dead fox was draped around her shoulders. She was sitting on a chair that had a back made of thin round wood that curved into the seat. The seat was round, and too small for her large bottom. The whole chair looked very weak and incapable of managing to support such a weight. It strained under the large frame of the well-endowed customer. She moved slightly on the seat and it groaned. The queue gasped! Lindy giggled. Cludgy gave her a look telling her to stop. The large lady, with her shopping complete, left the shop by squeezing through the rather small door.

It took a while to get to the head of the queue and buy their groceries. Delays occurred when the item a customer wanted wasn't available, so they had to choose another one.

'Choosing can take time,' said Cludgy.

With their purchases Lindy and Cludgy went to Ray's the greengrocers, where there was a bigger queue. At the front was the large lady with the dead fox around her shoulders. They had no chair for her there. Out of the shop, Lindy asked about the dead fox. 'That's horrid, why does she wear it?'

'Because it's fashionable, or was before the war,' Cludgy answered. 'She's quite a wealthy woman, but with all her money she can only buy the same amount as she's allocated because of the rationing and shortages.'

The biggest queue was at Tomson's the butchers. They had to wait half an hour, as the queue went down the high street. They did manage to get three sausages and some liver. 'Enough for two meals,' said Cludgy. 'Liver makes lovely gravy,' she added.

Once the shopping was done their two baskets were full. Lindy carried the meat and some of the vegetables, and Cludgy carried the rest. They walked down Union Street to the Esplanade to get the bus there. There was a toy shop at the bottom of the hill and, although Lindy looked in, there was nothing to interest her at all. 'It's all too expensive in any case,' she said.

They walked along the front and kept noticing little bits of burnt paper.

'What's all this paper?' questioned Cludgy.

Lindy picked up a couple of pieces and tried to read what was written. 'Nothing makes sense, they're all different,' she remarked.

'They've come over from Portsmouth,' said a voice from behind. 'They didn't half take a battering last night.'

Further along the Esplanade they reached the train tunnel. They heard first and then saw the steam train come puffing out. Cludgy and Lindy were too near and they disappeared covered in smoke.

The Ryde Pavilion Theatre was just across the road. It suddenly crossed Cludgy's mind that looking across the Solent at Portsmouth after last night's raid would not be a good idea. 'Shall we go now? I've had enough and I'm a little cold,' suggested Cludgy.

Lindy didn't hear, as she had already started to walk around the theatre to the sea wall. She leant over it and looked across the Solent. Evidence of the raid was still there. Smoke could be seen hanging over the city.

'There must be small fires still burning!' she said.

Seeing Lindy's solemn face, Cludgy said, 'Let's go home, and have a nice cup of tea. I've enough flour and fat to make some jam tarts. Shall we fill them with the blackberry jam you helped me make last summer?'

Their walk to the Esplanade meant they had to pay an extra penny to travel that extra distance. 'Never mind, I love to see the pier and the sea,' said Cludgy.

However hard Cludgy tried, there was little reaction on Lindy's face. 'Cludgy, I feel that life is full of nothing

247

nice!' she said. 'It's all horrid and hateful.'

'It will change, I promise. You're due some good fortune, I'm sure.'

They got on the bus, sat down and the conductress took the fare.

'When I get home, I must finish my letter to Daddy,' she said.

'You could write about the lady with the dead fox!' suggested Cludgy.

'And that poor little chair!' Lindy said. 'How it managed to support her, I'll never know.'

'I wonder what would have happened if the chair had given up and collapsed on the floor?'

Lindy's sense of humour returned. 'I now know what to write to Daddy. I'll write him a story about Sarah the chair and her encounter with Mrs Plum and her large bottom.'

'Lindy! I'm shocked at such language!'

'What else should I call it?'

'I don't know. Does it have a happy ending?'

'I'm trying to think of one. Mrs Plum could lose weight? Or Sarah the chair could be sympathetically mended and retired to live in peace in the back room of the shop, where the shopkeeper's wife, a slim lady, sits on it daintily!'

'Yes, I like that one,' enthused Cludgy.

The story was written and the letter was posted.

For days, there was no letter for Lindy. Every

morning she watched the post lady arrive, expecting one from her father. Every day there was nothing, and every day Cludgy had to think of a reason why there was no letter to soften the disappointment. 'It's the war, lots of letters go astray.'; 'Maybe he's very busy.'; 'It may be lost.' And 'He'll write another one, I'm sure.'

'He usually writes within two days of any raid, and he hasn't written,' said Lindy.

'Be patient,' said Cludgy.

'Oh, where is he Cludgy?'

A few days after the raid, people in the village were talking about Lindy and her father, and how they wrote to each other a lot.

'She writes about her life in Little Bridge,' said the postmistress, 'and he draws pictures in his letters back to her.'

In the Post Office one day, Peggy Vaughan was posting her letter to her fiancée Brian, who was also a fireman in Portsmouth. People behind her were talking about Lindy and her father.

'She hasn't heard from him since that raid last Friday,' the postmistress continued.

'Poor little lass, she must be so worried. Surely, they would have told her if he was missing or injured. They've been very busy since that awful raid. Maybe they haven't had time.'

Peggy, ever full of tact, said, 'I wonder who he has put down as next of kin.'

'I suppose they couldn't have put down Lindy, she's only ten years old,' the postmistress continued.

'I know what I'll do,' said Peggy. 'I'll write to Brian again, and ask him to make some enquiries, he's a fireman in Portsmouth.'

33
Mishaps, Misdirections and Misunderstandings

William Elliot woke up in a hospital bed. He was totally disorientated.

'Where am I?' he said to a nurse who was passing his bed.

'Hey, hello. You're awake!' she said.

'Awake but where?' said William.

'This is not the first time you've woken up; you've been in and out of consciousness a couple of times,' the nurse explained. 'You did give us your name, although no surname. When you were admitted, the ambulance just dropped you off. You came in without a name, but they did tell us briefly what happened in the burning house.'

William wasn't listening. He looked around - it was obviously a hospital. 'In hospital but where? Am I in Portsmouth?'

'You're in a hospital in Winchester. I'll go and tell sister.' The nurse scurried off and disappeared down the long corridor of beds. All were full of men who had bandages on various parts of their bodies, and there were two with legs in plaster that were hoisted up on a frame above them.

'William is awake,' she told the sister.

'Gosh, that's good,' she said. 'Go and sit with him, I'll be over in a minute.'

'Why Winchester?' he asked the nurse when she

251

returned.

'Because Portsmouth hospital was full. Do you remember what happened to you?'

'I think there was a bulldog!' ventured William as he racked his brain to try to remember.

'I don't know about a bulldog, but I do know you had a knock on the head. Despite being trapped by a load of debris; you were not too badly injured anywhere else.'

William turned his head toward the nurse. 'The silly woman was going to use a stirrup pump on a fire that was burning furiously.'

'William you're beginning to remember; that's good,' said the nurse. She was silent when she took his pulse. 'A stirrup pump?' she continued. 'Was she really? I wasn't told that!'

'We couldn't do anything for the Guildhall, you know,' William said. 'Such a dreadful shame.'

'I know,' the nurse said sadly. 'It was totally destroyed; such a pity. It was a magnificent building.'

The sister arrived and read the chart where the nurse had recorded his pulse rate. She checked his eyes with a torch, flashing them in and out of each eye and watching the pupils. 'Can you tell us your full name?'

'My name is William Elliot,' he paused. 'I can't remember the number of my station, but my section commander is Geoff ...' and here he stumbled again. 'Sorry, I can't remember.'

'Not to worry. It will come back to you soon.'

Then William suddenly said; 'You've a torch. I had a torch! I shone into the back room: the blackouts were up; it was pitch black. Then I saw two eyes staring at me. They belonged to a stout and angry bulldog. Gosh, he was big and frightening.'

'Your colleagues found you on the floor pinned down and almost buried by debris!'

'That awful dog knocked me over!'

'There was an explosion when you were lying on the floor. It brought the ceiling down, and the lumps of plaster that fell almost buried you as you lay there. It must have been a piece of ceiling that knocked you out.'

'Knight!' he shouted. 'That's his name: Geoff Knight.'

'Your mates had a devil of a job rescuing you. As they were digging you out, ashes and debris from the fire upstairs fell down on them. Your face and eyes were saved as you had ...'

'I had my arms covering my face,' William interrupted.

'That's right,' said sister. 'It's all coming back, but not all in the right order.'

'They put your helmet over your face and dragged you along the corridor and out of the building. You were lucky, very lucky that the firemen got you out in the nick of time. The top floor collapsed just as you were carried through the front door. There was apparently nothing left of the house.'

As the nurse came round later on that day to take his

pulse and temperature, he continued to tell her what he remembered.

'We had to find a water tank and a fire nearby! The mains had been bombed,' he said. 'That'll be a good story to tell Lindy.

Lindy!' he shouted, 'Oh my goodness, how long have I been here?'

'You came in on Friday night, and it's Tuesday today.'

'Has anyone told Lindy?'

'Who's Lindy?' asked the nurse.

'My daughter - she's on the Isle of Wight.'

'I'm told your section commander informed your next of kin,' said the sister. 'You came with all that information but they omitted to tell the ambulance men your name. It was you who told us on Sunday that it was William. Today you've told us your surname, Elliot. The sister wrote it down on the chart and admission form.'

'Oh, my goodness, my next of kin! That's Aunt Joan,' William put his head in his hands. 'She knew that Lindy was evacuated. But she wasn't given an address. She won't know where she is, and Lindy won't know where I am!'

---oOo---

During the previous June, just after the evacuation of Dunkirk, Aunt Joan decided to evacuate herself. The war had got more intense.

'I can afford it,' she told her neighbour Mrs Rooney rather haughtily. 'There's no reason why I shouldn't move

254

away from here.'

'No reason at all,' the neighbour replied.

'I am going to a lovely place in the country,' she pontificated, 'to stay with an old school friend. She is now Mrs Worthington,… er … or is it Wallington?'

She handed over the address. It was written in pencil on a small piece of paper and folded over in the middle. Mrs Rooney opened it up to read it.

'Would you do me the greatest of service,' said Aunt Joan, 'and forward my post to my new address, please?'

'Yes of course I will,' said the neighbour. She glanced at it briefly, noticed there was an address written on it, folded it again and put it in her desk.

Aunt Joan didn't get many letters, in fact, none at all. In her usual officious manner, she had informed her bank and other important official correspondents that she was moving, and had passed on the address to them. However, the piece of paper with Aunt Joan's address on it remained in her neighbour's desk and was thought of no more, until a letter arrived for Miss Joan Elliot on Monday 13th of January. The postwoman knew that Miss Elliott had moved away and knocked on the door of the next door house.

'Do you know where I can find Miss Elliot?' she asked.

'Yes, I do, I've her address in my desk,' said the neighbour. 'Leave the letter with me and I'll post it on to her.'

The letter was in fact from Geoff Knight, William's

255

station commander. Mrs Rooney found the piece of paper and picked it up. She squinted at it. She took it to the window for a better light then she found a magnifying glass. Mr Rooney, her husband, looked closely at it too. She then realised just how badly it had been written. 'Oh, how I wish I'd checked it with her when she was here,' she said.

'Is the name of person who is her host, a Mrs Worthington or Wallington? I don't think she knew, as when she told me she was moving she couldn't remember.'

Mr Rooney had no idea either. 'We'll just have to guess!'

'Is the house number a number three or an eight?' Mrs Rooney sighed.

'It's Church Street, that's clear enough, but there must be thousands of Church Streets throughout the country,' Mr Rooney remarked, 'and look at the way the name of the village is written, it's awful. Is it Honley or Haniley?'

'Stupid woman,' Mrs Rooney said, 'She didn't add a county.'

It was all guesswork, but they could do nothing else. Mrs Rooney wrote what she could decipher, and they posted it. The letter was not seen again until it was returned to Geoff Knight six weeks later.

---oOo---

In the meantime, after receiving Peggy's letter, fireman Brian Drawbridge went to his section commander after his shift, explained what had happened and that he wanted to find William Elliot, also a fireman in Portsmouth. After a few phone calls and visits, they found William's station, and Brian went to see Geoff.

'Whilst I make some enquiries,' Geoff suggested, 'you go to every hospital or medical centre you can find and do the same. He may turn up there. None of the lads here knew where he was sent to. We knew he was alive and unconscious, but we know no more.'

Brian took to his bike and together with a map went all over Portsmouth searching for a fireman who might have been admitted on Friday. He had no luck at all. Then he had a brain wave! 'I'll ask at the ambulance stations, someone must have taken William to hospital,' he said.

He was right: someone remembered a fireman without a name going to a hospital in Winchester. 'We knew the story of this man and how he got his injuries, but we had no name,' the ambulance man said. 'His mates did say that they would deal with informing next of kin and any other paper work.'

'A simple thing like a name, and it got forgotten,' said Brian. 'Thank you anyway. I'm off to Winchester.'

Brian cycled to Winchester and found a small hospital which pre-war had been a private country house. He found a woman behind a desk by the door.

'Have you had a fireman called William Elliot

admitted here?' asked Brian. 'He came in last Friday. The ambulance men had no name for him.'

'We were very busy on Friday,' said the woman on reception. 'Very busy indeed! Rushed off our feet we were. There was no time to take names. The doctors and nurses were totally occupied trying all they could to save lives.'

'**Busy!** So was I!' Brian was a little tired by now. 'I've come from Portsmouth. I too was very busy fighting fires in Portsmouth on Friday. The man I'm looking for is a fireman who was also fighting fires and who also came from Portsmouth!'

Immediately the woman behind the desk sat up. 'I will make some enquiries for you. Would you like to sit down and wait?'

Brian had not heard all that the woman said, but he did pick up the phrase 'sit down and wait'.

'No! I would not like to sit down and wait,' said Brian. 'I'm going to stand here until you've exhausted all your enquiries. He's in here; the ambulance man told me.'

Brian was directed to Ward C, where William was sitting up supported with pillows. A bandage was around his head.

'Are you William Elliot?' Brian asked tentatively.

'Yes,' he replied.

'My name is Brian, and my fiancée is Peggy Vaughan, and as a member of the Red Cross she escorted Lindy Elliot to live in Little Bridge on the Isle of Wight.'

William was shocked, surprised and overjoyed to hear the news.

'You'll have to speak clearly, I'm deaf.'

William sat up, and started to shout.

'No good, I can't understand shouting, just speak clearly please.'

Brian sat down on a chair given to him by a nurse. William spoke directly and clearly to him. The two men talked about their experiences of Friday's raid. William explained how they were directed to house fires that were near water supply tanks. Brian too had been fighting house fires using water from the tanks.

'Awful!' said Brian.

'Just awful!' agreed William.

'I can write to Peggy and tell her we've found you.'

'No, no, that's not quick enough. I want to get over to the island; Lindy must be so worried. Will you help me, Brian? I need to get to Little Bridge and see Lindy for myself. I've not been able to get a letter to her. Please, you must help me.'

'I have some leave,' Brian continued, 'just a couple of days, and I was going over anyway to see Peggy. I'll take you, but you do need to have a permission letter.'

'I had one to visit her in December, we could use that.'

'Do you still have it?'

'Yes, it's in my jacket pocket over there.'

Brian went to the jacket and found the precious slip

259

of paper.

'Look, it expired on the 1st of January,' said Brian.

'Bother, it's out of date,' said William.

'Not if you put a three in front of the 1st!'

Brian took out his pen, fortunately filled with matching black ink, and squeezed in the important number three before the 1st. 'There,' he said admiring his handiwork, 'look, you have a permission letter valid until the 31st of this month!'

Brian went back to thank Geoff Knight and to report on William's recovery. 'Do you know if Lindy, his daughter, has been informed of the accident?' Brian asked.

'I understand that Miss Joan Elliot, his sister and next of kin, would have done that,' he replied.

However, Joan Elliot **hadn't** received the letter, and consequently no-one had informed Lindy.

34
Just a Walk

Betsy Brown knocked on the door;

'Come in,' called Cludgy from the kitchen stove. She was cooking porridge for Lindy's breakfast. She served it up to Lindy, who added the honey.

'Reggie has rather a rotten cold this morning, so I'm not sending him into school today.'

'Nothing serious, I hope,' said Cludgy.

'Oh no, I'm sure he will perk up soon. He's rather exaggerating his blocked nose and headache at the moment,' Betsy continued. 'Mind you, when I said he could miss school today, his whole attitude changed. I'm sure I saw a smile.'

'That sounds like Reggie; so he's not dying, but hopes that you're convinced that he might if he doesn't have a day off school.'

They both laughed. 'Anyway,' continued Betsy, 'Lindy, could you please hand in this note to Miss Simons? It explains why Reggie is not in school today.'

Lindy finished her porridge, put her packed lunch into her school bag, picked it up and took the letter, which she slipped into her pocket. She stepped out of the kitchen door and began her walk on her own to school.

It was now a week since the big raid on Portsmouth, and still there had been no letter from her father. She had written three times to him. She tried to think of valid reasons for this but couldn't. They always acknowledged each other's letters. She was sure if her letters had gone missing, he would have sent another one anyway.

She got to the end of the lane. In front of her was the main road where the buses ran. Coming along down the hill, she met Rosemary Manners. 'Hello Lindy,' she called out.

And then in a flash, she had an idea. 'Hello Rosemary, could you please hand this letter in to school? I've an errand to do.' Rosemary took the letter, crossed the road and started to walk up by the cemetery to the school. Lindy stayed on her side of the road. Rosemary turned and waved just as Lindy turned left and walked towards Ryde.

At this point she hadn't got a plan. She didn't know where she was going or how long she would walk. In her satchel she had her small, packed lunch. *That'll be enough for the day,* she thought.

She passed the golf course and laughed to herself remembering Reggie putting golf balls into the policeman's saddle bag on his bike.

She opened the gate to Spencer Road and walked on towards Ryde. *I feel so lonely*, she said to herself, *and yet I've Cludgy and Arthur to go home to. But where's my daddy?*

When she got to the Esplanade, she realised that perhaps she had gone far enough and that she should return home now. The burnt pieces of paper that littered the pavement and road last time she was there had mostly all gone. There was the odd piece caught up in a hedge or brambles to remind her of that awful night.

I'm sick of being brave, she said to herself. *I'm fed up with people telling me I'll be alright; I am not being alright, it's awful.*

Cludgy had made her a cheese sandwich for her lunch, and had added an apple. She ate her lunch seated on the wall, looking at the pier. In this cold quiet day, it was easy to hear the tram rattling along the pier bringing passengers to Ryde. She remembered her ride with Peggy Vaughan. Her daddy had arrived via the pier and so had Reggie. *I wonder whether they caught the tram when they arrived on the island, or perhaps the children marched down the long pier,* she pondered. *I don't know if Daddy caught the tram that day. I wonder if I will ever know? Oh, how I wish he could walk down there now, and I could run up to him and hold him tight,* she thought. She watched the tram rattle up and down collecting and then disgorging its passengers in front of where she was sitting, again and again. She folded her arms across her body and cuddled herself. 'And if I was holding my daddy, I wouldn't let him go!' she said out loud. 'AND NEVER LET HIM GO!'

She carefully folded up the greaseproof paper in which Cludgy had wrapped her sandwiches. She would want to use that again on another day. 'Waste not, want not!' she said, mimicking Cludgy. She ate the apple right down to the core; checked it for any flesh she may have missed and nibbled it away. Then she threw it onto the beach where the seagulls were resting. They squawked and screeched as they fought over it. 'Sorry, seagulls, I should have brought more apples.'

As she started her walk back to Little Bridge, she

pulled her hat further down over her ears, and checked her scarf was in the best place to keep her neck and chest warm. She was feeling colder. 'I'll walk faster, that'll warm me up,' she said.

At the bottom of the hill in Ladies Lane, she realised that she was yards from her favourite place, the beach. Something within her urged her to go there. It was not the welcoming place it had been in the summer when the sun beat down on their bare arms, legs and sandalled feet. It was grey, dismal and the sand was cold when Lindy sat down in her much-loved spot. She thought of Pieter and wondered where he was now. 'Safe, I hope,' she said out loud. 'He was such a nice man.' She started to shiver, but she wasn't ready to face going back to the cottage just yet. She drew her knees up to her chest and cuddled them.

She imagined herself back in August when the sun was shining, Reggie was jumping over the stream and getting his shoes wet. Strangely she had stopped shivering, her muscles became stiff and she began to feel warmer. Tired, she lay down, her eyes shut, and she disappeared into her dreams of Reggie, Pieter and her father.

35
Getting There

It was eleven in the morning when William was finally free of the hospital in Winchester. Brian had organised boat tickets. They made their way to the main road to Portsmouth. 'We'll hitch a ride from here,' said Brian. 'The roads aren't very busy, but I'm told that the military use this route frequently. Maybe we'll be lucky.'

Luck was on their side, and a Bedford 3 tonner lorry, full of soldiers, pulled up. 'Where you going?' asked the driver.

'Portsmouth!' yelled Brian.

'Hop on then. What part of Portsmouth?'

'The Harbour,' they both replied.

'We're going to the Isle of Wight,' said William.

'Taking a holiday?' quipped the driver.

'Hardly!' said William.

'I can drop you off at Portsmouth Harbour.'

'What a service! Thank you very much'

Seeing William's bandaged head, two soldiers put out their hands to help. Brian gave William a leg up into the back of the lorry and the two soldiers helped him to get over the tailgate.

'Here mate, you sit over there on the bench,' instructed another soldier.

'My friend is deaf but can hear you if you look at him and speak clearly,' instructed William.

Brian deftly manoeuvred himself into the lorry and sat down on the floor. 'Where are you all off to?' he asked.

'We don't know,' said one of the soldiers, 'and if we did know we'd not be allowed to tell you.'

'I'll give you a hint!' said Brian, turning his head left and right in a mock search for any German spy. 'We're going to Portsmouth.'

'I worked that out for myself,' said another soldier. 'I know the area. We've just passed Winchester, so I thought if we continue to go south east, we must hit Portsmouth.'

'I hope we stop in time,' joked a young lad, 'or we might fall in the sea!'

'You're firemen, aren't you? I hear Portsmouth was busy last Friday night,' enquired a soldier.

'Yes, we are firemen, and yes, it was!' said William.

'Standing holding a hose and fighting fire while the bombs are raining down isn't a job I'd like,' said the youngest-looking of all the soldiers.

The others agreed. 'That's not all we do! We rescue people as well,' said William.

Most of the soldiers were young, their uniforms looked new, and it struck William that they really didn't know what they were going into.

They arrived at the Harbour and the driver yelled out 'Next stop the Isle of Wight! All passengers to Ryde must alight here!'

Two soldiers lowered the tailgate and William and Brian slid down onto the road. They thanked the driver, swapped 'good luck' messages and made for the ferry entrance.

'If I'm going too fast for you,' said Brian. 'Let me know and we can slow down.'

'Oh no, I'll keep up!' said William. 'I'll be happier when we get onto the ferry.'

There were so many people in one uniform or another that Brian and William in their firemen's kit waited in the queue for the ferry unnoticed. Brian held the tickets and the permission letters.

'Your uniform!' commented Brian, 'has seen some action!'

'Yes, that was mainly due to that dog. I'll remember that animal all my life. He knocked me over!'

'You were beaten by a dog then?'

'Yes, that bloomin' animal! A bulldog; hefty thing it was, knocked me flat on the floor!'

The tickets were clipped, the letters were glanced at, and they simply walked through the barrier. No-one questioned the permission slips. Brian was holding them both. He had sensibly tucked William's behind his.

'Our brave firemen! Hooray for our brave firemen!' shouted the ticket collector. 'Well done, you deserve medals for the work you did for the city last Friday.'

'Just doing our job!' said William as they walked on and up the green gangplanks.

268

'You alright?' asked Brian.

'Yeah, fine now! We're nearly there.'

Despite the cold, the two men found a sheltered place on deck. William couldn't face crowds in enclosed places at that moment.

At Ryde Pier Head they took the tram the length of the pier, where they were again and again praised by all and sundry for their work on controlling the fire on the 10th of January.

'Is it really a week ago?' commented William, turning towards Brian to speak.

'Yep! A whole week. It was a vicious raid.'

'It's coming up to the anniversary of my wife's death. Another reason to get to Lindy as fast as we can.'

'I don't think this tram knows that fact,' joked Brian, as they chugged along slowly to the Esplanade.

A bus took them to the bottom of Little Bridge Hill, where they got off and walked down the lane towards the cottages. There was a lady in front of them, and she too was walking as fast she could. Unused to the speed, she puffed and coughed as she walked, sometimes breaking into a little run. Brian and William kept up with her at a steady pace. They turned at the church and saw the lady go into Cludgy's driveway and knock on the same door that they were going for.

Cludgy was getting tea ready when she answered the door. 'Hello Mrs Manners,' Cludgy said, 'what can I do for you?'

269

36
Together

'I think I've something important to tell you,' Mrs. Manners said, as she gasped for breath. She flopped down exhausted on to one of the kitchen chairs.

'Rosemary my daughter, you know my daughter don't you Cludgy?'

'Yes, of course.'

'Well, Lindy wasn't in school today. At the bottom of the hill, Lindy handed Rosemary a note to give to Miss Simons and then she watched as Lindy walked along the main road towards Ryde.'

Cludgy was shocked! 'That letter was about Reggie. That's not like Lindy to play truant! Whatever was she thinking? Where on earth was she going?'

'I can't help you there. Can I have a sip of water please?'

Cludgy turned to the sink, picked up a glass and filled it with water. Just as she was handing it to Mrs. Manners, William knocked on the kitchen door. Cludgy opened it.

'William! Brian! Hello!' she exclaimed. 'What are you doing here?'

'I've come to see Lindy.' William said smiling. 'Is she back from school yet?'

The look on Cludgy's face was enough for the two men to forget the usual pleasantries and listen to Cludgy's news about Lindy.

'That's the problem!' said Cludgy. 'She didn't go to school to-day! Perhaps Mrs. Manners, you could explain what your daughter saw this morning.'

Mrs Manners recounted her tale again.

'Wherever would she go?' said Cludgy. 'Come on think, think hard.'

'Could she have gone to the beach maybe?' suggested William. 'She took me there when I was down last.'

'Yes, yes,' said Cludgy excitedly, 'she loves the place because she can see Portsmouth from the shore.'

'Did she see the fire?' asked William.

'I'm afraid she did. She ran off down there and I had to go and get her.'

With William's help Brian managed to understand what was going on.

'We must get down there as soon as we can!' said Brian.

The two men left the kitchen and ran down the hill. Texi, who had been aroused by all the chatter from his slumber in the sitting room, was ahead of them. He chased straight down the lane to the beach. He found Lindy easily and barked incessantly.

Brian got there next. 'Lindy!' he called out. He gently shook her shoulders. 'I've found her William! She's here! Lindy! Lindy! Open your eyes!' Her breathing was slow and shallow.

Even with Texi's continual barking Lindy did not

271

respond in anyway. Her eyes remained shut and her body was lifeless. Brian felt her face, hands and legs. For a moment William just stood still, shocked as he looked down on his precious daughter.

'She's freezing cold!' said Brian as he quickly took off his jacket and wrapped it around her. 'We got to get her warmed up.'

'We must get her back to the cottage,' said William.

'I'll carry her,' said Brian as he picked her up and put her over his shoulder in a fireman's lift. 'I can be quicker holding her like this.' Brian carrying Lindy's lifeless body started back along the path and up the steep hill. Texi again ran ahead, barking all the way. In his shirt sleeves, Brian ran as fast as he could carrying Lindy's dead weight over his shoulder. William tried to keep up, but still suffering from his injury he followed at a walking pace.

Halfway up the hill, Brian saw Cludgy coming towards them. 'Get a kettle on,' he shouted gasping for breath, 'and then run around to the first aid post in Pitts Lane and get Peggy. She said she would be there sorting out equipment.'

Cludgy already knew what to do. 'The kettle's on,' she shouted back. 'I've just lit the fire in the sitting room. Mrs Manners is already on her way to get Peggy.' Cludgy had already put a blanket on the fireguard to warm.

Brian went straight to the sitting room. With his jacket wrapped around her he laid Lindy on the floor. 'We're going to need some more blankets.' Cludgy ran upstairs, and grabbed more from the linen cupboard.

The first blanket was warm; she handed it to Brian, who laid it over Lindy. She replaced the blanket on the fireguard with an extra one she had got from the linen cupboard.

William joined them puffing and panting; he took his coat off. 'Do you need another jacket?' he asked.

'No, I've got some blankets,' said Cludgy. 'Leave the coat on her for the moment, sit in the chair and hold her close to you; your body heat will help, we need to warm her slowly.' Brian laid the blanket over Lindy and William.

Nearly in tears, William held his daughter close to him. 'Lindy, Lindy darling, wake up,' he kept repeating.

Brian lifted a further blanket from the fireguard and laid it over the first one.

Peggy arrived! The story was told.

'We must get some warm liquid into her,' said Peggy, 'Is she at all responsive when you call her?'

'No, not yet,' William replied.

'She is hypothermic,' said Peggy.

'Cludgy, could you get a warm drink ready for me please? I'll give it to her with a spoon,' instructed Peggy.

'I've got some milk, and I'll add some honey, that's her favourite!'

Peggy took off Lindy's lace-up shoes and started to gently massage her cold feet. A further blanket was ready warmed. 'Let's lift her up and put it underneath her.' Brian carefully lifted her as Peggy laid the blanket on

273

William. Peggy then wrapped her up and laid the first two blankets back over them both.

William continued to talk to her 'Lindy darling, it's time to wake up! Come on Lindy!'

All of a sudden Lindy said, 'Hello Daddy!' The room fell silent. But that was all Lindy could manage as she lost consciousness again. William increased his call to her. 'Lindy, Lindy, wake up! It's time for school!'

Lindy opened her eyes and said, 'Are you an angel, Daddy? You have a halo!'

'That's my bandage,' he replied. However, this was not heard as Lindy fell asleep again.

A few minutes later she said, 'Are we in heaven, Daddy? Could we go and look for Mummy now?'

'That's better,' said Peggy. 'A long sentence! Let's try and give her the warm milk and honey now.'

Carefully and slowly Cludgy spooned Lindy's favourite warm drink into her. Colour started to return to her cheeks: and her hands and feet began to come back to life.

Slowly and surely Lindy's consciousness improved. 'Keep talking to her, William,' said Peggy, 'and include questions she has to answer. She needs to stay awake until she's totally warmed up.'

William thought for a minute and then he said, 'I met a dog called Pickle.'

Lindy opened her eyes. 'Where did you meet him?' she said.

'In a house in Portsmouth. He was owned by Mrs Withers. Do you know what the silly woman was doing when we found her?'

'No! What?'

'Well, the top half of her house was on fire, and she was in the kitchen. She was filling up a bucket of water. Do you know what she was going to do?'

'Put the fire out,' said Lindy

'Yes, how do you know? You weren't there!' teased her father.

Lindy smiled. 'What was the dog doing?' she asked.

'Guarding his property,' replied William. 'We got her out of the building and then I went back for Pickle.'

'What sort of dog was he?'

'As I said his name was Pickle, and he belonged to the old lady. What sort of dog do you think he was?'

'A small one?'

'Well, that's what I thought! He wasn't! He was a large fat bulldog. He knocked me over. Beaten by a dog! That's nothing to be proud of, is it?'

'Keep it up, William,' said Peggy, 'She's beginning to recover. I must watch the clock, the sirens could go off at any time soon, and then I'll need to get back to the first aid post.'

'I say William, have you got anywhere to stay tonight?' asked Brian, 'I'm sure my Auntie Maud would be willing to give you a bed.'

'I hadn't thought of that at all. My only thoughts

275

were to get to Lindy.'

'I've already made your bed up,' called Cludgy from the kitchen' 'I guessed that you would want to stay with her.'

'Thanks all the same, Brian. And thank you for your help today, I couldn't have managed without you.'

'Oh yes, I mustn't forget.' said Brian as he searched in his pockets. 'Your permission letter, I must give it back to you. You might not get off the island without it. I'm leaving tomorrow afternoon; I'm on duty at six pm. You'll have to go back on your own.'

'Permission letter! You managed to get another one,' said Cludgy, 'with such short notice?'

The two men looked at each other rather sheepishly!

Cludgy looked at the two grown men. They were like two schoolboys who had just got caught robbing a tuck box. 'What have you been up to?' asked Cludgy.

'Nothing!' said William.

'It was just a little adjustment!' said Brian.

The two men bowed their heads in mock shame! Suddenly there was a knock on the door.

'Hello,' shouted Reggie, 'can I come in please?'

'Yes Reggie, come in, ... oh, I see you're already in!' said Arthur.

'I heard that Lindy wasn't well, so I had to come round.'

'You've made a remarkable recovery from your illness of this morning Reggie,' remarked Cludgy. 'How did that happen?'

'Oh yes,' he coughed as he put his hand on his throat. 'I wanted to show Lindy my picture I painted today.'

He held it up proudly.

Reggie's captive audience admired the picture. 'Getting the perspective right was tricky!' he said. 'Auntie Bee taught me all about that. Things further away look smaller,' he remarked with an air of authority.

'Do you know,' said Arthur, 'that picture is really jolly good? Look, Cludgy.'

Cludgy agreed. Brian and Peggy looked over Cludgy shoulders at Reggie's work of art. 'You've painted a fine picture,' said Peggy.

'An artist in the making,' agreed Brian.

'Lindy, you can have it if you want,' offered Reggie.

Lindy and her father looked closely at the picture. 'It's my beach!' said Lindy. 'Look Daddy, that's the stream that Reggie jumps over every time we go there, and he always gets his feet wet!' Reggie smiled.

'And that's where I sit when I go there,' Lindy continued.

'Yes,' said William, 'that's where we found you today.'

Cludgy made tea and there were a few homemade biscuits to share around. The room was warm and there was lots of chatter. Peggy and Cludgy shared biscuit recipes. Arthur and Brian talked about fishing. Brian added that he belonged to the Ryde Rowing Club.

'Perhaps when all this is over, we could go fishing together,' said Brian. 'I'll row you out to St. Helen's Fort. There's often a good stock of mackerel swimming there.'

Lindy, her father and Reggie talked about the beach. They all agreed that it was much nicer in the summer. As time went on Lindy's colour in her cheeks returned, her feet and hands were warm. She began to talk more and joined in the conversation.

It was very dark when Peggy and Brian left hand in hand. 'I wonder when they'll marry?' said Lindy. Arthur and Cludgy went to the kitchen, leaving Lindy with her best friend Reggie and her father watching the embers in the fire.

She pulled up the blanket closer to her chin, and cuddled up to her daddy.

'Are you alright?' he asked.

'Yes, I am alright!' she said.

About the Author – Jo Cooper

This is Jo's second book. Her first Isle of Memories was a biographical snapshot of her childhood on the Isle of Wight during the 1950s and 1960s. A Red Sky is a further venture into her youth, although not witnessed the second world war, she has extensively researched the period at that time. The characters in the book mirror the activities of some of her family and friends during her childhood. Her father Brian Drawbridge experienced the massive fire in Portsmouth on the 10th January, 1941. Her mother saw the red sky it created.

Before her retirement to the Isle of Wight, Jo was a successful swimming teacher and tutor. Jo has been married for 53 years, has two children and three grandchildren.

Printed in Great Britain
by Amazon

84314986R00163